The Da[rk]
(Matt Dra[ke #35])

By
David Leadbeater

Copyright © 2024 by David Leadbeater
ISBN: 9798323751310

All rights reserved.
No part of this publication may be reproduced, distributed, or transmitted in any form or by any means, including photocopying, recording, or other electronic or mechanical methods, without the prior written permission of the publisher/author except in the case of brief quotations embodied in critical reviews and certain other non-commercial uses permitted by copyright law.

All characters in this book are fictitious, and any resemblance to actual persons living or dead is purely coincidental.

Classification: Thriller, adventure, action, mystery, suspense, archaeological, military, historical, assassination, terrorism, assassin, spy

Other Books by David Leadbeater:

The Matt Drake Series
A constantly evolving, action-packed romp based in the escapist action-adventure genre:

The Bones of Odin (Matt Drake #1)
The Blood King Conspiracy (Matt Drake #2)
The Gates of Hell (Matt Drake 3)
The Tomb of the Gods (Matt Drake #4)
Brothers in Arms (Matt Drake #5)
The Swords of Babylon (Matt Drake #6)
Blood Vengeance (Matt Drake #7)
Last Man Standing (Matt Drake #8)
The Plagues of Pandora (Matt Drake #9)
The Lost Kingdom (Matt Drake #10)
The Ghost Ships of Arizona (Matt Drake #11)
The Last Bazaar (Matt Drake #12)
The Edge of Armageddon (Matt Drake #13)
The Treasures of Saint Germain (Matt Drake #14)
Inca Kings (Matt Drake #15)
The Four Corners of the Earth (Matt Drake #16)
The Seven Seals of Egypt (Matt Drake #17)
Weapons of the Gods (Matt Drake #18)
The Blood King Legacy (Matt Drake #19)
Devil's Island (Matt Drake #20)
The Fabergé Heist (Matt Drake #21)
Four Sacred Treasures (Matt Drake #22)
The Sea Rats (Matt Drake #23)
Blood King Takedown (Matt Drake #24)
Devil's Junction (Matt Drake #25)

Voodoo soldiers (Matt Drake #26)
The Carnival of Curiosities (Matt Drake #27)
Theatre of War (Matt Drake #28)
Shattered Spear (Matt Drake #29)
Ghost Squadron (Matt Drake #30)
A Cold Day in Hell (Matt Drake #31)
The Winged Dagger (Matt Drake #32)
Two Minutes to Midnight (Matt Drake #33)
The Devil's Reaper (Matt Drake#34)

The Alicia Myles Series
Aztec Gold (Alicia Myles #1)
Crusader's Gold (Alicia Myles #2)
Caribbean Gold (Alicia Myles #3)
Chasing Gold (Alicia Myles #4)
Galleon's Gold (Alicia Myles #5)
Hawaiian Gold (Alicia Myles #6)

The Torsten Dahl Thriller Series
Stand Your Ground (Dahl Thriller #1)

The Relic Hunters Series
The Relic Hunters (Relic Hunters #1)
The Atlantis Cipher (Relic Hunters #2)
The Amber Secret (Relic Hunters #3)
The Hostage Diamond (Relic Hunters #4)
The Rocks of Albion (Relic Hunters #5)
The Illuminati Sanctum (Relic Hunters #6)
The Illuminati Endgame (Relic Hunters #7)
The Atlantis Heist (Relic Hunters #8)
The City of a Thousand Ghosts (Relic Hunters #9)
Hierarchy of Madness (Relic Hunters #10)

The Joe Mason Series
The Vatican Secret (Joe Mason #1)
The Demon Code (Joe Mason #2)
The Midnight Conspiracy (Joe Mason #3)
The Babylon Plot (Joe Mason #4)
The Traitor's Gold (Joe Mason #5)

The Rogue Series
Rogue (Book One)

The Disavowed Series:
The Razor's Edge (Disavowed #1)
In Harm's Way (Disavowed #2)
Threat Level: Red (Disavowed #3)

The Chosen Few Series
Chosen (The Chosen Trilogy #1)
Guardians (The Chosen Trilogy #2)
Heroes (The Chosen Trilogy #3)

Short Stories
Walking with Ghosts (A short story)
A Whispering of Ghosts (A short story)

All genuine comments are very welcome at:

davidleadbeater2011@hotmail.co.uk

Twitter: @dleadbeater2011

Visit David's website for the latest news and information:
davidleadbeater.com

The Dark Tsar

CHAPTER ONE

Soroyan was angry, simmering like water in a boiling kettle. He poured himself two measures of vodka, lifted the glass and downed them immediately. Then he poured himself two more, still savouring the burn. He dallied with the next two, staring introspectively across his office. All the blinds were drawn. It was a dark evening and stars and moonlight and shit like that didn't really move him. Besides, he enjoyed the solitude, liked being alone. Especially when he was seething.

He rose and paced the length of his office, did it again and again. His heart was already beating fast. He was a fit man, slim and tall and possessed of a bald pate that gleamed under several bright lights. His eyes were black coals and his mouth a thin red line. At the moment, it was almost white.

He was waiting. The time was almost here. He glanced at the wall clock – almost nine. Good. He sipped at the vodka. Soroyan had a one-track mind, and that track followed whatever was in front of him. Tonight was one of the biggest nights of his life.

To pass the time, he wondered how many men and women he'd had killed through the years. Too many to count. And did it really matter? Of course not. Soroyan was just impatient. He picked up his phone, scrolled for a few minutes. After that, there finally came a knock at the door.

'Yes?'

The door opened, a familiar face thrust through the gap. 'They are ready.'

At last. Soroyan nodded, refilled his glass, and, clutching it in his left hand, made his way out of the office. He went down a flight of stairs, turned left and followed the wooden panelling to the end of a long corridor. There, he stopped and opened a door. Inside was a large office space.

The space bristled with an array of chairs, all facing a dais. The chairs were filled with men and women, all capable, all loyal – his various captains. They sat up expectantly as he entered the room. Soroyan walked directly to the dais.

He took a deep breath, calming the anger. He needed to be succinct here, to the point. And they needed to understand the importance of what he was about to say. Indeed, he thought. There was nothing more important.

Tension lay across the room. These were his captains, the men and women who carried out his instructions across the length and breadth of his criminal empire. They delegated the day-to-day tasks – they were essentially the beating heart of his organisation. And here they were – all gathered together. Something that had never been done before.

How should he best approach this?

'Listen to me,' he said, his voice a low rasp. 'Some of you will be aware of the operation in Prague, some won't. Basically, we snatched a politician's daughter and demanded a ransom. When that ransom didn't initially come, we... enhanced... the request. We gave the man a deadline. We waited... and we waited,' he took a long breath. 'A decision had to be made. We decided to cut our losses and, of course, to save face, teach the man a lesson.' He waved a distracted hand. 'Of course, this is standard procedure. She was never getting out in one piece, anyway.'

There were several hard smiles and nods among his audience. Everyone knew what happened to kidnap victims.

Soroyan cleared his throat. 'I tell you this information, this story, for a very good reason. For it is now that a new player enters the game. Have any of you heard of a company called Glacier?'

Blank looks and the shaking of heads greeted his question.

'Glacier is a private security firm operating out of Washington, DC, and Los Angeles. They provide services for various firms operating in dangerous locations. You know the type. Ex-soldiers, mercenaries. Protection. Enforcement. That kind of thing. They also appear to operate under the radar.' He paused.

More blank looks and frowns.

'This politician did indeed want his daughter back. He maybe even knew our policies. For this reason, he contacted Glacier and arranged his own hostage rescue team. He hired a bunch of people to come rescue his daughter.'

'They attacked the house?' Someone ventured.

Soroyan somehow tethered his anger. 'They did,' he nodded. 'A six-person team raided the house where we were keeping the daughter. They hit hard and fast, highly experienced.'

'Did they get the daughter?' Someone else asked.

Soroyan slammed a fist into the wall behind him. 'That is not the point,' he said, looking out over the audience. 'The daughter is no longer the point. Don't you see? It's the *house.*'

He saw dawning knowledge in several eyes.

'The house,' a woman said. 'Of course.'

'It was a mistake to use the house,' Soroyan said. 'But we've never had problems before,' he shrugged. 'So it was never an issue.'

'I'm assuming these Glacier mercenaries did more than rescue the girl?' A shrewd man asked.

Soroyan bit his lip until it bled. 'Look,' he said. 'I want you all to have the full picture here so that you can make better decisions when I give you your tasks. The house where we took the politician's daughter is an important headquarters. Prague is second only to *this* HQ. There are a lot of very important documents there.'

Again, he paused, gauging the room. He took a big gulp of vodka before going on.

'There is one large office, one large safe. Glacier entered the house, killed the guards and rescued the daughter. Then, because they are mercenaries and always on the lookout for any kind of plunder, they noticed the safe. They'd already killed our guards, so they had the house to themselves. It seems they took a little time to crack open the safe.'

His audience was on tenterhooks. They were all wondering what might be so important inside the safe. Soroyan himself could barely believe he'd been so stupid. But it was just complacency. He was secure in his world, his criminal enterprise, his violent kingdom. Always, he was surrounded by capable armed guards. Not just his person, but his home and grounds. He had felt entirely safe about his empire too, certain that nobody would dare invade his space.

'What was in the safe?' Someone ventured.

Soroyan knew he hadn't spoken for a while. He was too angry. Now he took a deep breath, gritted his teeth, and then tried to move forward.

'Listen,' he leaned forward. 'The safe held an incredibly important document that the mercenaries recognised and stole. These Glacier bastards not only rescued the daughter, but they stole from me, too. Yes, it was an opportune theft, but it really couldn't be any worse.' He shook his head. 'It really couldn't.'

You could hear a pin drop in the room. Everyone was leaning forward.

Soroyan sighed deeply. 'The sensitive document was a list of my money stashes and bank accounts throughout the world. I've always called it my 'stash list.' It holds details of countries, amounts, currency, addresses. It's comprehensive, ridiculously so. But you need to know where your assets are, right?' He shrugged. 'The stash list was kept in a leather wallet inside the safe and, now, it's missing.'

'And it held everything?' Someone asked with disbelief in their voice.

Soroyan nodded. 'It is exhaustive. With it, a person or perhaps an authority could find all my accounts, my liquid assets, my personal stash. They would know how much there is in each place. And they could go right to the very location.'

As he'd expected, there was a stunned silence in the room. No one wanted to say anything. No one wanted to express their disbelief in a tone that might get them into trouble. Soroyan felt defensive.

'A record had to be kept,' he said shortly. 'I can't be expected to remember everything.'

He realised he was sounding too apologetic and rallied. 'These bastards,' he said. 'This Glacier scum. They stole from us. They took something of great importance and left us with nothing but a big fuck you. They violated our inner circle. We have to do something about this. Not only do we need the document back, we need to teach them a lesson. They have to understand that you don't attack the Soroyan syndicate and get away with it. You pay for your actions in fresh blood.'

His audience was reacting, nodding vigorously, getting that violent light in their eyes. They were twitching as if they wanted to strangle the very life from the next innocent person they saw. Soroyan liked the reaction.

'What's the plan, boss?' Someone asked from the back.

'The plan? It's threefold. First, you should know that the man in charge of Glacier is named Connor Bryant. He's a hands-on kind of guy, apparently, so I'm sure will have known all about the operation. And he's got the stash list, too.'

'How could you know?' A woman asked.

'I have a spy in his office. As you know, I have snitches in many companies across the world. It helps our business go round. The more the merrier. My contact in Bryant's office tells me it's a source of amusement that Bryant now has in his possession a list of a major criminal's accounts and stashes.' He shrugged. 'That's how they tell it, anyway. Bryant hasn't kept the fact quiet.'

'Is he part of the plan?' Someone asked knowingly.

'Threefold,' Soroyan repeated. 'First, and most importantly, we retrieve the stash list and any copies that may have been made. We have to do this quickly before Bryant stops gloating and hands it over to the authorities.'

'Do we know where it is?' someone asked.

'Our spy has all that covered. Now, secondly, we make Glacier pay. As an organisation that has wronged us, they should not step away from all this unharmed. Thirdly... Connor Bryant.'

The audience gave him a collective knowing smile.

'He will pay, too. And badly.'

CHAPTER TWO

Mai Kitano woke to find sunlight streaming in through the curtains. Had they overslept? A quick glance at her watch told her that no, they hadn't, and it was going to be a beautiful day.

She rolled over. Bryant lay at her side, still asleep and snoring gently. This was a big day for him, she remembered. Glacier was opening another satellite office, this one in Madrid, and he was excited about it. Another step, another expansion. Glacier was global now, expanding every year.

Mai stretched and gave him a shake. Her midnight black hair splayed across his pillow. Bryant woke to find her inches from his face and smiled.

'That's nice,' he said.

'Talk like that might get you laid first thing in the morning.'

Bryant smiled, and then a look of panic entered his eyes. 'Oh, damn, I don't have the time.'

Mai could have made a crack about two or three minutes but held it in. Instead, she nodded. 'Today's the day,' she said. 'Madrid.'

'I have to get moving,' he said.

'Maybe another office will bring in more jobs,' Mai said. 'We've been pretty quiet since taking care of the devil's reaper.'

Bryant shuddered. 'Don't remind me. That was a rough one for you. And, hey, don't worry. I'm sure something will come along soon.'

Mai and her team, these days known as the Ghost Squadron, had worked for Bryant and Glacier ever since leaving government employment a few years ago. The jobs had been sporadic and had made them rent properties in Washington, DC. Before Glacier, Mai and Drake and the others had barely finished one mission before falling straight into another. These days, the work was a little quieter. A fact that had good and bad connotations for the team. On the one hand, they had more spare time. On the other, they weren't quite as sharp, quite as focused. It was a double-edged sword, and Mai still wasn't sure what lifestyle she preferred.

'The devil's reaper was definitely rough,' Mai said. 'The last couple of weeks of peace and quiet have helped put it out of my mind.'

Bryant swung his legs out of bed. 'I'm sure something will come along soon. Maybe via Madrid.'

She nodded, conscious that his mind was elsewhere and not really concentrated on her. She didn't blame him. This was a big day.

'You want breakfast?' he asked.

'Do you have time?'

'Breakfast or sex,' he said. 'What's your fancy?'

'I do love a good muffin,' Mai said. 'But you choose.'

Bryant checked his watch. Mai already knew what he'd say. 'Let's grab a coffee,' he said. 'And then I have to go.'

They rose together, dressed, and headed for the

kitchen. Bryant put the coffee machine on and Mai grabbed a couple of croissants out of the cupboard. They sat at the breakfast bar and drank and ate whilst Bryant constantly checked the time.

'I'm sorry,' he said, realising what he was doing. 'You don't deserve to be treated second best.'

'I understand,' he said. 'Today's different. And we're good,' she hesitated. 'We're good, aren't we?'

Bryant blinked at her. 'Of course,' he said. 'Solid. Why would you ask? Have I done something wrong?'

Mai smiled, knowing they were both slightly insecure. Bryant had had to create a brash outer exterior to go farther in business, to fit in with certain expectations, and this hadn't led to good relationships. Mai had had several good relationships but had never actually settled down properly with anyone. Was it her fault? She didn't know.

'In any case,' Bryant went on, finishing the last of his coffee with a gulp. 'The whole firm's quiet at the moment. I have several teams not working.'

'The world doesn't need private security at the moment,' Mai said.

'It seems so. How is your team handling it?'

Mai suppressed a smile. 'As expected, I guess. Dahl's champing at the bit, always eager to get involved in something. Hayden and Kinimaka are taking it in their stride, keeping busy. Cam and Shaw are taking the time for themselves. They have a lot of barriers to cross, but are still together. Kenzie... well, she's just Kenzie. Brusque. Sarcastic. On it... all day long.'

'And Drake and Alicia?' Bryant asked.

'Taking it day by day. They're desperate for action,

but know how to keep a low profile when they have to.'

Mai bit her lip at that point. Recently, there had been talk about the team branching out, about them creating their own private security firm and working for themselves. So far, it was all talk. Nobody had seized anything by the horns and made a proper decision. Mai felt bad about keeping the proposal from Bryant, but whilst it was just that – a proposal – there was no point causing any upset.

The suggestion, though, the idea, was what was keeping Dahl from going out of his mind with all the inactivity. He was researching it deeply, getting an idea of what things had to be put in place, of what qualifications might be required, of what great contacts they had who could help them get started. He was on it in a big way.

Which only made things harder for Mai.

She looked at Bryant now and smiled. He was getting ready to go. Now was definitely not the time to bring anything important up.

'I'll see you later,' she said, picking her white leggings out of a pile of clothes.

'You going to the gym?' He asked, shrugging a jacket on.

'I don't do gyms,' Mai said.

He pointed at the leggings. 'So why?'

'I do *boxing* clubs,' she said. 'Places where you can kick some ass and stay sharp. That's where I'm going.'

'Oh. Well, have fun.'

'You too.'

She reached out to hug and kiss him. Bryant held

her tight, longer than he should have for a quick goodbye. His lips were close to her right ear.

'Never worry about if we're good or not,' he whispered. 'You mean the world to me.'

'Am I 'the one'?' She smiled.

'Very much so.' She felt him smile and then, as expected, his insecurity kicked in.

'Am I the one for you?'

'For now,' she grinned, and then gave him a punch in the ribs. 'Stop it. I don't get that mushy. You know that.'

'But...'

'Look, Connor Bryant, and listen. I'm here with you. You have me. I'm the happiest I've been in a long time. You mean everything to me. Is that enough for now?'

He gripped her. 'For now.'

She watched as he walked towards the door and opened it. 'Hurry back,' she said.

'Oh, don't you worry. I will.'

Mai started preparing her boxing gloves.

CHAPTER THREE

When the team arrived in Washington, DC, they saw they had one hour of daylight left and went immediately to the darker suburbs of the city. They were twelve strong, composed of men and women, all capable and tough and deadly. There was a look about them, a no-nonsense, severe air that said they were killers. By the time darkness had fallen, through contacts, they had bought enough weapons to take Glacier off the map and several other items that might be needed.

Their leader, a man named Preston, didn't have to say much, didn't have to show his authority. This was a crack team, the best that could have been assembled. Every man and woman knew their job inside out. This suited Preston. He was taciturn at best. They stowed their new purchases in their rental cars and drove to a hotel. They would spend the night before hitting Glacier tomorrow.

Preston thought about the upcoming mission. There had been no time for a proper surveillance of the premises, so they did not know what to expect. Of course, there would be guards, but Preston had total faith in his team and knew they'd be able to take them out. And there would be civilians too. Not an issue. If they got in the way, they would die. The only wild card would be if one of Bryant's various teams was on site. That might cause a few issues.

Preston was a worrier, a quiet worrier. He overthought every mission. Treble checked every detail. He never let on how anxious he became, but never let it upset his performance. The team followed his every order implicitly, and that was enough. Preston was confident with them.

Now they parted. They knew they had to be at the highest level tomorrow, so only three of them headed for the bar, and Preston knew that would only entail a couple of drinks at the most. The rest headed for their rooms, to chill, to rest, to sleep. Preston himself also headed for his room, as happy as he could be the night before a potentially lethal mission.

What had Soroyan said?

First, the Stash List. That was essential. It had to be returned and they would do anything in their power to get it. The snitch they had in the office had given them a location... unfortunately it was on the top floor in Connor Bryant's own office. On hearing that, Preston had just shrugged. If it was a simple mission, he wouldn't be involved.

Second, they were supposed to teach Glacier a lesson. To Preston's mind, this would involve fucking up their offices, their infrastructure, maybe an employee or three.

Third, and potentially most difficult, they had to teach Connor Bryant a lesson. They couldn't be sure the man would even be on site, but they had his picture and, if he was there, they would act accordingly.

Preston reached his room, thoughts swirling

around his head. He inserted the card reader and entered, stowed his gear. He ran a glass of water, sat down on the bed, and sighed. Preston hadn't killed anyone in weeks. Tomorrow, he thought, would be fun.

The next day dawned bright and crisp and sunny. Eight o'clock became nine and then ten. Washington, DC, basked under balmy skies, its citizens going about their daily business. Outside the offices of Glacier, other establishments bustled – the baker's shop with its queue out the door, smelling of fresh bread and pastries. The coffee shop doing a brisk trade with its displays outside the windows. There was a jewellery shop and a fashion store and a couple of office buildings, and it gave a snapshot of everyday life in DC. Glacier itself was a glass fronted white stone building about ten storeys high. There was no sign of a guard out front or directly inside the lobby.

Preston was hyped up to the max. Three cars pulled up to the front of Glacier's offices and stood idling at the kerb. The driver stayed in each car, ready for a swift getaway. The other occupants all piled out, guns in hand, masks on their faces, Preston included. They raced across the concrete space to Glacier's front doors and then pushed inside. Preston was the first to enter the lobby.

Ahead stood a curving wooden reception desk. Several people stood behind it, eyes wide, faces momentarily slack. Preston's immediate concern was for guards. He saw one immediately, stationed by the elevators to the right. Making his intentions clear,

Preston aimed his gun and shot the man in the chest. The shot echoed through the lobby.

People started screaming.

They ducked down behind the reception desk. They started running through the lobby, crawling towards the far staircase. It turned into bedlam. Preston's team didn't take part in it. They were focused. Two of the team fired for effect into the wall above the desk, shattering paintings and wall lights. Timber and glass rained down across the people sheltering behind the desk.

Preston waited for just a few seconds. Now, they would leave a man behind to slow down the attempts to call the cops. This man would roam the lobby, take charge, and get very vocal. He would put the fear of God into them.

This man knew his place and started vocalising now. Preston ran to the elevators, jabbed at the button. His comrades ran with him. They waited for the car to return to the bottom, guns at the ready. Behind them, the solitary merc ran to the reception desk and pointed his gun behind it, shouting harsh words. When he saw a man headed for the staircase, he shot that man in the back, grazed a couple of others with bullets. These civilians had become hostages now, and they were under intense threat.

The elevator arrived, doors sliding open. Preston glided in; his team filling the space. They hit the button for the top floor and waited. Preston readied his gun, feeling slightly incongruous, counting the floors as they rode to the top. The ride lasted just a minute or so, and then the doors slid open once more.

They leapt out, guns up. An open-plan office space lay before them, people sitting at their desks typing, eating, on the phone. Several eyes widened as the mercenaries jumped out of the elevator.

More screams.

Preston swept his gaze across the room. Some people were standing, mouths agape. Others were scrambling away. More were seeing the situation and responding. Preston saw the closed doors at the far side of the room and started running towards them. His team, capable and professional, didn't start shooting right away. They wanted the occupant of the far room – if there was one – to be on the lowest alert level possible.

Preston hit the doors hard, sending them slamming back into the room. He stepped through, finding himself in a large corner office with windows that looked out on two sides of the city. Nice. The desk was rectangular and mahogany and covered in folders and piles of paper.

And behind the desk sat Connor Bryant.

'What do you want?' he asked.

'We want the Stash List!' more than one man yelled.

Preston waited for his team to join. They left another merc behind to subdue the people in the office, to stop them from contacting the authorities. Preston felt and saw his team fan out around him.

He pointed to the desk, to the stack of folders on the left-hand side. There, they would find a tatty looking brown leather wallet. Preston could see it right now, on top of the pile. He waited as one man went around the desk to claim it. The man leafed through quickly, nodded, and shoved it into his jacket.

'The Stash List,' he said loudly and with satisfaction.

Bryant watched, hands in the air. 'You work for Soroyan?'

'You stole from the wrong people,' Preston said, his voice a soft drawl. He didn't enjoy talking, but felt like he had to say something.

'I had no control over that,' Bryant said. 'Sometimes mercenaries go off mission.'

Preston nodded. 'You should control them better. This time, their misjudgements have destroyed you.'

'You're welcome to the leather wallet. I didn't know what to do with it, anyway.'

'Have you shown it to anyone?' Preston thought to ask. He waved the gun at Bryant's head menacingly.

'No. I haven't even got my head around it yet. As I said, I can't decide what to do.'

Preston believed him. The wallet had been sitting in a casual manner, just laying on top of the pile. It certainly looked as if Bryant hadn't finished with it yet.

Time was wasting. Preston had already succeeded in two of the three tasks Soroyan had set them. They'd retrieved the wallet, given Glacier some payback. That just left the issue of Connor Bryant.

The man didn't look scared. He was just sitting there with his hands in the air, casual and unafraid.

Preston said, 'You really pissed Soroyan off.'

'The wallet wasn't part of the plan. I told you. The mercs fucked up.'

'They were working for you. You bear the

responsibility.' Preston wondered if he should mention the politician's daughter, who they'd also rushed to safety.

Preston didn't want to waste any more time. His orders were explicit. Make Connor Bryant pay for his actions. He raised his gun, took aim.

'No,' Bryant said quickly. 'I didn't-'

Preston pulled his trigger three times, shooting Bryant twice through the chest and once in the middle of the head. Bryant's lifeless body slumped in the chair.

Preston turned away. 'Let's get out of here.'

CHAPTER FOUR

Mai returned home from her daily bout at the boxing gym and took a shower. She changed and made a coffee, sitting at the breakfast bar in Bryant's home, staring out the window across the building landscape outside. There wasn't a lot to see except for walls and windows and the back ends of houses, so she soon grew bored. It was ten thirty a.m. She wondered if she should call Bryant. Maybe they could decide on what they would do that night.

She was just about to refill her cup when Hayden called her mobile. Mai answered immediately.

'Hi,' she said. 'Everything ok?'

'Yeah, yeah,' the American said. 'I'm just getting bored with all this inactivity and… well…'

'Thought you'd pump Connor's squeeze for information?'

Hayden laughed. 'I didn't think of it *that* way but, yeah, I guess you're right. Has he got anything coming up?'

'He's totally focused on opening up the new office at the moment. Told me he has a few teams inactive. I think we'll be cooling our heels for a little while longer.'

Hayden sighed. 'Is it quiet out there in the world? Bad guys taking extended vacations?'

'We don't work for the government anymore. We don't have their reach.'

Hayden sighed again, sounding thoroughly frustrated. 'I guess so. Well, keep me informed, won't you?'

'You'll be the first to know.'

Mai was about to end the call when her phone started buzzing. She saw the call was coming from Glacier HQ.

'Hey,' she said. 'Hold on, I'm getting a call from Glacier. Might be what we're looking for.'

'That's strange,' Hayden said. 'I'm getting a call, too. So is Kinimaka.'

Mai's brow furrowed. It suddenly all felt very odd. She ended the call with Hayden and jabbed at the other one.

'Hello? This is Mai.'

'Mai? It's Steve Redding.' This was Bryant's second in charge. She wondered why he was calling her.

'Steve? Is everything okay?'

'I... I'm afraid not. There was an attack on the HQ just now. Mercenaries. They shot up the place, shouting about some list. They had guns, Mai. Machine guns.'

'Shot up the place? Jesus, is Bryant okay?'

Steve didn't answer her. The line was very cold and, suddenly, frightening.

'Is Bryant okay?' she asked again.

Steve's voice shook as he spoke. 'They killed him, Mai. They shot Connor dead in his office.'

Mai sat heavily, the phone feeling like a block of ice in her hand. Her mouth went dry, her heart missed a beat. She couldn't speak, couldn't think, couldn't comprehend what Steve was telling her.

'Bryant... is...' she managed.

'I'm so sorry. We're all... all in shock.'

Mai didn't know what else to say. She stared at the far wall, not seeing it, not seeing anything. Her legs were jelly, her face slack.

'What do you want to do?' Steve asked.

Mai couldn't answer. She told him she'd call him back, then just sat without moving. She stared into space; the shock coursing through her system. Many times, she had confronted death. Several times, her own friends had been killed. But this was different. This was entirely more personal. She couldn't move, couldn't make a sound.

Time passed. Mai stayed in position. She still held the phone. It rang again, but she didn't even look at the screen. Emotions were boiling through her, yet they left her as cold as ice.

Eventually, there came a knock at the door. Mai was surprised, and the noise brought her out of her daze. She looked over to the front door and saw a shadowy figure standing outside — more than one. Without wondering who it could be, with no safety in mind whatsoever, she put one foot in front of the other until she stood next to the door.

Then she pulled it open.

She barely registered the people standing outside. She heard Drake's voice and then Hayden's. They were all there. The entire team. Either someone had rung all of them or they'd called each other. It was Hayden who held out a hand to steady Mai.

'I'm so sorry.'

They went back into the house, wandered to the living room. They stood there, staring at each other, expressions of shock on their faces.

Drake spoke first. 'Listen up, people. Our friend has been murdered. Does anyone have any information?'

'Shot in his office,' Kinimaka said.

'At least eight shooters with top-flight weapons,' Dahl said.

'Killed some of the staff, too,' Kenzie said. 'Wounded others. Shot up the whole HQ.'

Alicia made her way over to Mai. The Englishwoman put a hand on her friend's shoulders. 'I'm so sorry, Mai.'

The Japanese woman nodded. She tried to focus, to get past the grief. This wasn't the time to wallow — it was the time to take action. Mai's central core couldn't look at it any other way. It was how she was built. The grief would have to wait. She simply had to *do* something to temporarily get past it.

Talking helped.

'Something about a list,' she said, her voice raspy. 'They were looking for a list.'

'It's all too sketchy,' Shaw said. 'We really need to get down there.'

Mai looked at her and nodded. 'You're right. We need to be at the scene, to talk to witnesses. We need to fully understand what's happened.'

She knew why she felt that way. She wanted to understand everything surrounding Bryant's death as much as she possibly could. And the only way to do that was to visit the scene of the crime.

The entire team made its way down to Glacier HQ.

They arrived together and started making their way to the front doors that were currently cordoned off with yellow crime scene tape. Mai peered through the front windows and saw Steve Redding in the lobby.

She took a moment to call him, saw him walk up to the window and then ask one of the uniformed officers if they could come in. The officer nodded and held the door open for them. Mai and the others joined Steve in a far, quiet corner of the lobby, surrounded by potted palms.

'What the hell happened, mate?' Drake asked. 'Why is Bryant dead?'

'Why?' Redding looked at him. 'Because some heavily armed assholes forced their way across the lobby, rode the elevators, and then smashed into Bryant's office in a matter of minutes. They killed all the security along the way, took no casualties. They were good, damn good. A crack team. Witnesses overheard a couple of them shouting about a Stash List. It seemed highly important to them. Once they had it, they killed Bryant.'

Mai swallowed heavily as he spoke. She looked up. 'Is he up there now?'

Redding bit his lip. 'Yeah, they haven't moved the body yet. Still working the scene, I guess.'

'They killed him after he gave them the list?' Shaw said. 'Which tells me that's what they came for. But if that's the case, why kill Bryant and the others?'

'They were pretty liberal with their shooting, but they didn't just cause a bloodbath,' Redding said. 'They could have, easily. But they held back.'

'They came to make a mess,' Cam said. 'But not too much of a mess.'

'Any ideas what this list might be?' Drake asked.

Redding shrugged. 'There's no CCTV in Bryant's office, so I can't tell you what was taken and if I've been read into it. I do know Bryant was given a list recently by the team that saved the politician's daughter in Prague. Bryant couldn't decide whether it was a good or bad thing. The mercs had fucked up stealing the list, but Bryant then said it could potentially be a boon. He couldn't make his mind up.'

'He didn't call it the Stash List?' Mai asked.

'No. But it's the only list I know of in recent weeks. That's how he referred to it, anyway. Some kind of money storage list.'

'Is it still there?'

'I'd have to check.'

'Maybe you could do that?' Drake said. 'If it's gone, we have a good idea of what we're looking for.'

Redding nodded and headed across to the elevators. Five minutes later, he was back down. 'I spoke to the investigators,' he said. 'Told them I might be able to identify what was missing. They let me look.'

'And?' Dahl asked.

Redding nodded with surety. 'They took the list I mentioned. It's definitely no longer where it was.'

'Then that's where we'll start,' Drake said.

CHAPTER FIVE

Matt Drake tried to put the grief out of his mind and focus on the task at hand. Bryant had been killed for a reason, and this Stash List was clearly of utmost importance to someone.

They were still standing in the lobby, unchallenged. Steve Redding had wandered off elsewhere, and now the team stared at each other.

'I feel ineffectual,' Hayden said. 'I feel like we should be doing something.'

'But what?' Cam asked.

'Up there in the office looking for clues,' Kinimaka said.

'That's not what we do,' Alicia pointed out.

'I used to,' Kinimaka told her. 'Kind of. So did Hayden.'

'We have all the clues we need,' Drake said quietly.

All eyes turned to him. 'Eh?' Alicia said.

'They made a point of killing Bryant,' Drake said. 'That tells us something. It tells us Bryant had a terrible enemy. He pissed someone off. And that means there's a connection. One we have to find.'

'And then there's this Stash List,' Dahl said.

'Exactly.' Drake shifted his weight. 'Look, we're no good standing around here, and we're starting to draw attention,' he nodded at the assembled cops, who were giving them suspicious looks. 'Let's go.'

They made their way out the front doors and back into the day. Weirdly, in the space of an hour, their whole life had changed, and they'd lost someone they cared about, and yet the day went on. The sun still shone as brightly as ever, the breeze ruffled their hair. People came and went about their business, and the bakers and the coffee shop were still bustling away. Nothing had changed... and yet everything had changed.

Drake led them to a bar. They found a corner table and ordered coffees all around. Nobody felt like eating. They sat in silence for a while, staring at the table as the surrounding noise and conversation passed them by.

'I feel shellshocked,' Kinimaka said, the big Hawaiian nursing a tiny drink.

Drake let out a long sigh of anxiety. 'It sure gets you,' he said. 'But this is when we have to focus.'

'On what?' Mai said listlessly. 'What can we possibly do?'

'On moving forward,' Drake said. 'There's something we have to do.'

'And that is?' Alicia asked.

'Make Bryant's killers pay.'

'You said something about this Stash List,' Dahl said.

Drake nodded. 'If you focus, it becomes clear. As I said, they killed Bryant for a reason. It wasn't just a random kill. And they came here purposely for this Stash List.'

'Makes sense,' Hayden said. 'But they left a big mess behind.'

'Depends on who did it,' Dahl said. 'They could be sending a message. Don't fuck with us, or we'll fuck with you big time.'

Drake nodded. 'Possibly. But to my mind, there's only one way forward.'

The others sipped their hot drinks, listening, trying to move Bryant's murder from the forefront of their minds.

'We focus on the Stash List,' Drake said. 'That's obvious. So what do we know about the Stash List?'

'The attackers wanted it above all else,' Dahl used his fingers to click points off. 'They engineered this whole operation around it. They knew – at least roughly – where it was.' He paused. 'Have I forgotten anything?'

'The most important thing,' Drake said. 'We reverse engineer the operation. We find out who carried it out by discovering *who the list was stolen from in the first place.*'

'And we do that how?' Shaw asked.

'By talking to the team that stole it,' Drake said. 'Bryant's team. The one that rescued the politician's daughter in Prague. They stole the list.'

'It might be in Connor's records,' Mai looked out a window toward Bryant's office.

'The cops'd never let us search,' Drake said. 'You know that.'

'So how do we find the team that stole the list?' Dahl asked, but looked confident, as if he already knew.

'We use Redding,' Drake said. 'He tells us where the team members are. We go on a flying visit. We talk...' he spread his hands. 'And we have a target.'

'We're gonna avenge Bryant in cold blood?' Hayden said uncertainly. 'That's not what we do.'

'He was my friend, my lover,' Mai said quietly. 'He meant the world to me.'

'Someone shot him in cold blood,' Cam said. 'That deserves retaliation.'

Drake held his hands up. 'I'm not saying we go in all guns blazing. But I am saying we have to track Bryant's killers down. Maybe bring them to justice, teach them the errors of their ways. I am saying they should pay for their sins.'

'We find them,' Alicia said. 'For Bryant.'

Drake nodded. 'For Bryant.'

'And when we do?' Hayden pushed it. 'What then?'

Drake shrugged. 'I guess we assess the situation, love,' he said. 'We make a spot decision, like we often do. I can't say how that will play out.'

Hayden looked at each of them, assessing the expressions on their faces, the lights in their eyes. She nodded. 'I have an idea how that will turn out,' she said.

Mai whirled on her. 'Are you kidding?' she snapped. 'These bastards killed Connor. And you're advocating for leniency?'

Hayden shook her head. 'All I'm saying is we have to be careful. We kill someone in cold blood and we're as bad as they are. And we could end up in jail.'

'Don't worry,' Dahl said quietly. 'We can keep it all under the radar. Whatever we do,' he added.

Drake finished his drink. 'So, is everyone agreed? We talk to Redding again and then this other team?'

'And then we find them,' Alicia said. 'And get them to talk.'

'Don't worry,' Drake said. 'They're on our side.'

Alicia looked at him. 'You should know by now, Drakey. Nobody's really on our side. Not outside this team, anyway.'

Drake saw the hard years of living in her words, the betrayals, the near misses with death. He knew the place her words came from because he felt the same way.

'Well, they're as close as can be to friendlies,' he said. 'We shouldn't have any trouble.'

Dahl snorted. 'Us? We're trouble magnets.'

Drake couldn't disagree. 'I kind of agree with you there,' he said, and then shrugged. 'But what else can we do?'

He rose to his feet. There seemed to be a consensus among the team. Hayden, Kinimaka, all the others, tended to agree with him. That was all Drake needed. The only way to confront most problems was to move forward, to pile drive over them, to put them behind you. This was Drake's preferred method.

He pulled his phone out. 'I'm calling Redding.'

CHAPTER SIX

Drake shifted in his plane seat, uncomfortable. The plane food sat before him, looking quite tasty for a change. Alicia, beside him, had already attested to the fact, and he was looking forward to it. He tucked in. The flight had two hours to go.

They touched down with a squeal of rubber and a woosh of air-brakes. The plane taxied to the terminal and then they were inside, heading through the gates and looking for a large taxi. Soon, they were winging their way through the dark concrete streets of another city, in another town, anonymous, ordinary, indistinctive, just one more built-up American metropolis where one man awaited them.

They had connected with the leader of the Prague team and had agreed to meet him in a nondescript café in the centre of town. The taxi took them there now, depositing them at the kerbside, and then sped away. Drake was left staring after it, wondering about the twists and turns of fate that put men and women in a particular place at a particular time. Bryant could have been on holiday, at the sandwich shop, on the toilet, or running late, but he had been sitting right there behind his desk when the bad guys broke in.

Fate.

He spotted the café they were looking for and led his team towards the front doors. Inside, it was roomy and airy, with plenty of tables and space between them. Drake looked around and immediately spotted a potential candidate for the team leader in a far corner.

He walked up to the man, received a nod in return.

'Jake Butler?' he asked.

'That's me. Take a seat. I didn't realise there would be so many of you.'

Drake blinked, and then realised the guy was probably right. The size of their team didn't really occur to him anymore, but it might actually come across as intimidating.

'You prefer to talk to just me?'

'Just a couple of you. How's that?'

Drake nodded. Both he and Hayden took a seat at Butler's table whilst the others sat across the room. They ordered drinks and pastries and then sat back to do business. Drake watched Butler all the time. The man's eyes were in constant motion, always assessing the room and any fresh faces that entered the café. It was second nature to him, and something he couldn't hide. Butler was the real deal.

'So you lead a team for Bryant?' he began with.

Butler nodded. 'We call it the 'A' team.'

Drake blinked. 'Really? That's original, mate.'

Butler shrugged. 'It wasn't taken.'

'We're the Ghost Squadron,' Hayden told him.

'Has a certain ring to it.'

Drake got down to business. 'So tell us about this mission in Prague.'

Butler stared at them for a long minute. 'Bryant's really dead?'

'Murdered,' Drake said. 'In cold blood. They made a point of doing it and, believe me, they didn't have to.'

Butler let out a long pent up breath. 'I can't believe it. Bryant always seemed so on top of things, in charge, you know? He was a good boss.'

'All the more reason to find out who killed him,' Drake said.

'And make them pay?'

Drake didn't look at Hayden. 'Maybe.'

'All right. Well, there was a politician whose daughter was kidnapped. A ransom was delivered, but this politician never thought the kidnappers would leave his daughter alive. He believed they'd take the money and kill her, anyway.'

'Probably correctly,' Hayden said.

Butler nodded. 'No doubt. Bryant asked us to go into the country, to find the girl and rescue her. So that's what we did. Took out all the bad guys and saved the girl. Brought her home to her father.' He sat back, looking content.

'But that's not all you brought out,' Drake said. 'Is it?'

Now Butler looked unhappy. 'The safe was right there in the next room. It was open. There were important looking documents, money, guns, files and wallets. We figured it couldn't hurt to get something over Soroyan. It would give Bryant a bargaining chip if he ever needed it.'

Drake nodded. 'Which is how you came to steal the Stash List.'

Butler nodded, hanging his head. 'I can't believe it got Bryant killed.'

'You couldn't know that would happen,' Hayden said. 'I get it. You were trying to help.'

Butler rallied. 'That's exactly what we were doing. Trying to be good soldiers, earning our keep.'

Drake cleared his throat. 'Whoever lost it was desperate to get the stash list back.'

'Soroyan,' Butler said.

'The Stash List is his?' Drake felt his heart beat faster as they got to the crux of the matter.

'Yeah, a guy called Soroyan. He organised the daughter's kidnapping, the ransom demand. He's very big in Budapest, a major criminal player. Most nasty things happening in that city go through him, one way or another.'

'So the Stash List belongs to Soroyan?' Drake pressed. 'It's his?'

Butler shrugged. 'Has to be. It was his operation we hit, his premises.'

'But he works out of Budapest. Not Prague.'

Butler nodded. 'All I know is what we learned during the op. This Soroyan is, chiefly, an arms dealer. But he dabbles in everything. He's big in Europe, based in Budapest. I guess he likes to branch out. He's into all the nasty stuff that you can imagine, including nukes if he can get them. Doesn't give a shit who he sells what to,' Butler sighed. 'He's one of those people we really wished didn't exist.'

'We've come across them before,' Drake said. 'More than our fair share, actually.' He didn't mention the Blood King or the Devil, the voodoo queen, or any of the other countless freaks and murderers they'd encountered.

'Soroyan may be evil,' Butler said. 'But he's well protected, well funded, and clever. Look how quickly he pulled the Bryant thing off. That should tell you how dangerous this man is.'

'Nothing we can't handle,' Drake said. 'And he will pay for what he's done. You don't walk into our world, destroy it, and then just dance on back out again. Doesn't happen. Soroyan will wish he never messed with Connor Bryant and the Ghost Squadron.'

Butler nodded. 'I wish you luck.'

'Any more info?' Hayden asked before they parted.

'Soroyan's quiet, not gaudy. He's not flash. He's a thinker, a planner. He surrounds himself with the best. The man comes from humble beginnings to the position he commands now. I'm sure you know – he's ruthless. A killer. The worst of the worst. He has no conscience.'

'He doesn't need a conscience to die,' Drake said.

Hayden looked over at him, but he ignored her.

'Shall we go to Budapest?' he said.

CHAPTER SEVEN

Drake was nothing if he wasn't direct. He wanted to leave Butler in the café, fly to Budapest, and go directly to Soroyan's hideout. And then, he wanted to confront Soroyan. After that, they would see where things led.

He directed the team quickly. They booked a flight to Budapest from the nearest airport to their homes in DC, grabbed their passports, went directly to the airport, and sat in the lounge. They were restless, anxious. It all seemed a little surreal. Here they were, on a revenge mission, flying across the world even as Bryant's murder scene was still being processed by the crime lab. They now had the lead, the man, the actual place where he made his headquarters.

This information had been provided by an eternally helpful source. Michael Crouch, Drake's old boss in the Ninth Division, a splinter group of the SAS, was incredibly well connected. He had contacts everywhere and in every agency, and it wasn't a stretch for him to get hold of someone high up in Budapest and find out where the famous criminal, Soroyan, made his base. The information came back in less than an hour.

Now they had the name and address of the man who had ordered Bryant killed. All they had to do was confront him.

Drake did not know how that would look. All he could think about was that they were all sitting in this airport under the bright lights, surrounded by the din of humanity, with just one goal in mind. It was fraught, crazy, ridiculous.

But they were doing it.

Their flight time came around slowly. They had been too pent up to eat. Most of them had downed a couple of drinks to help with the tension. Now, they boarded the plane that would take them to Budapest and sat down. They barely spoke to each other, all wrapped up in their own conflicts. It was most unlike anything that had come before.

The plane cut through the night, roaring them towards their destination. And confrontation. It landed hard in Budapest, bouncing down the runway and upsetting the passengers. This was Ferenc Liszt International Airport, and it seethed with activity. They hadn't brought luggage – no bags. They were in the same clothes they'd pulled on the morning Bryant died. It was a non-stop, hell-bent flight forward and, still, there was no time to waste.

Customs followed deplaning, and then they were out into the morning air. Every one of them walked quickly, taut with tension. They had no time to waste. The team rented a large car rather than using a taxi because they had some idea of what awaited them. The car rental seemed to take forever. Then, they were crawling in traffic, their lips thin red lines, their muscles hard, their fists clenched.

Inexorably, the stream of traffic took them closer and closer to their destination.

Now they were nearing Soroyan's base, Drake

knew they ought to be talking about it, trying to firm up some plan of action. But every time he opened his mouth to say something Bryant's face swam into his consciousness. He couldn't put the murder aside, couldn't get past it to focus on the present. Soroyan would pay. Oh, yes... that was going to happen.

The city of Budapest spread out all around them, vast, thick with civilians, busy. They passed high rises and office buildings, warehouses, and a housing estate. They entered the city proper and cut their way through. Soon, they were driving down a long road with car dealerships to the right and fields to the left. Drake saw signs for Mazda and Vauxhall and Porsche. The sat nav told him they were less than four minutes from Soroyan's address – the place where Michael Crouch's contacts had assured him Soroyan made his HQ.

Drake readied himself as the address came into sight. Straight away, he leaned forward and checked it out.

'At first glance,' he said. 'I don't like the look of that.'

It was a large, abandoned car dealership. The fence that surrounded it was old and tatty, the gates hanging askew. The building was worn, signs chipped and paled and broken. Some windows were just jagged teeth.

But there was a hive of activity. There were cars parked all around the parking area, men and women coming and going. Through the open doors and windows, they could see figures in constant motion. Drake wondered what they were all up to. Business was certainly brisk.

They pulled into a parking area across the street and lost themselves among the cars already there. This appeared to be a communal area, where workers left their cars and then walked to work. Through the dirty windscreen, they peered into Soroyan's area of business.

The activity didn't let up. Cars came and went. Everyone seemed to know what they were doing. Drake saw no sign of any guards outside, at least.

'There's something we need before we get settled down to do this,' Mai said.

Drake nodded. It was already on his mind. 'Drive,' he said.

Dahl was at the wheel. He knew what they had to do and where they had to go. Sensibly, he drove to a housing estate about three miles away and then made a call. One of Crouch's associates answered and gave further directions. The inside of the car was fraught with tension. They all wanted to act, not sit on their hands and wait. But this part of the plan was essential.

They followed the new directions, eventually ending up outside a tall block of flats that looked like it had some kind of disease, pockmarked front to back, its windows dark and grimy. In the car, Drake turned to the others.

'Who has the money?'

Hayden held out a bag. 'Everything's arranged.'

'Still, we should be careful.'

'Does it need all of us?' Cam asked, showing his relative inexperience.

'Just a few,' Drake said. 'Who's up for it?'

'I just want to get back to Soroyan,' Mai muttered aggressively.

Dake cracked open his door. Alicia and Kenzie went with him. Cam tried to follow, but Drake waved him back. 'Three is enough,' he said.

They left the car behind, walked up to the front doors, and pushed through. The elevator wasn't working. Litter surrounded it. In here, it was cold and stark, the concrete walls laden with graffiti. The staircase was all concrete. Their footsteps echoed up the stairwell, announcing their presence. All the way up and down they saw litter and old appliances, needles, towels, bedsheets and, once, even a mattress.

Drake entered the fifth floor, walked along the corridor until he found the right room, and then knocked three times. There was movement from within. The door opened. A man stuck his head out, black hair hanging long and lank. He eyed them lazily.

'Got password?' he muttered.

Drake blinked. Alicia stiffened beside him. 'We weren't given-' he began.

The lazy-eyed man started laughing and then flung open the door. 'Don't worry,' he said in heavily accented English. 'That *is* password.'

They were ushered through the door. Inside, the room was almost as bad as the stairway, so messy Drake could barely see the floor. A tall man with a bare chest sat on a sofa and a skinny woman leaned by the window. Both had guns in their hands.

'You here at Endo's recommendation?' the bare-chested man said.

It was the name Crouch had chosen for the transaction. Drake nodded. He said, 'Endo said you were good.'

The man inclined his head. 'You have the money?'

Kenzie raised the leather bag. 'Right here. Do you want to count it?'

The man leered at her. 'Of course I do. Trust is not all it is cracked up to be. Do you agree?' he started laughing, the woman laughing along with him. He waved Kenzie over. 'Put the bag on the table.'

Drake held a hand up to stall her. 'You have the weapons?'

The man licked his lips. He made no move at first, but then signalled to the woman. 'Fetch them.'

She turned towards a door, walked over and then gave a light knock. It was opened instantly by a man with a gun, this one fully clothed and wearing a brown leather jacket. He lugged in what appeared to be a very heavy bag and laid it on the floor close to the bare-chested man.

'Is everything there?' Drake asked.

'As close as we could get,' the man said. 'Now, the money.'

Drake bent down and unzipped the bag. He started inspecting the weapons as Kenzie handed over the money and let the man count it. After a while, there came a satisfied huff. 'It is all there,' he said.

'Of course,' Drake said. 'And the weapons are passable. Just.'

The bare-chested man shrugged. 'I had little time. Some of my men on the streets are going without weapons just for this. Just don't get caught with any of them.'

'They're well used?' Alicia guessed.

'Very well. You would be tied to many crimes with

them. And, of course, you would never mention me.'

Drake nodded. 'Then we're done.'

Two minutes later, they were leaving the block and returning to the car. It was as they hefted the heavy bag into the boot that the shadows slipped around them, guns in hand. Drake counted five of them, all dressed in black and with masks over their faces.

'Give us the guns,' one hissed.

'How do you know we have guns?' Alicia asked easily. 'Could be bottles of bourbon in there. Or cigarettes.'

'They know because they were told,' Drake said quietly. 'We're being double crossed.'

Slowly, the three of them spread apart. Drake heard car doors cracking open and knew his team was easing its own way out. The five black-clad shooters backed off slightly.

'Guns!' one yelled. 'Now.'

Drake made a show of reaching into the boot, playing for time. He saw Alicia and Kenzie take another step forward. To his left, Dahl and Hayden were getting closer to their opponents. Tension crackled in the air.

'Stop moving!' a man yelled, gun wavering. 'You need to-'

And that was it. The team's cue to attack. They hit hard and fast and devastatingly. Drake whirled at his man, striking the gun arm first, breaking the wrist. Alicia kicked out, disarming another and then followed up with a chin strike that practically broke his neck. Kenzie didn't hold back either, striking like a viper with stiffened fingers, blinding her attacker and then taking his gun.

Three down in just a few seconds.

The others were backing away, mouths open wide inside their masks, guns suddenly pointed at the floor. Dahl didn't hold back with his opponent. He lashed out, swiping the gun away, and then lifted the man by the neck, choking him. The man's legs kicked ineffectually until Dahl let him collapse to the ground. Once there, he gasped and writhed in agony.

The fifth attacker threw his gun down, turned, and ran.

Drake took charge. 'Quickly away, now,' he said. 'They'll be watching and might have more capable people.'

The team slammed the boot and then dived back into the car. Dahl started it and soon they were headed back the way they had come.

'All in all,' Alicia said. 'A very successful mission. We got the guns, and we had a bit of fun. I was hoping they'd renege on the deal.'

Drake nodded, face grim. 'Take us back to Soroyan's,' he said.

CHAPTER EIGHT

They waited for darkness to fall. For Drake, it was a tough few hours. All he could think about was Bryant's murder, and he could only imagine what was going through Mai's mind. The sun dropped lower and lower in the sky, and they surveilled the car dealership the whole time. Unfortunately, as the darkness started creeping across the land, they saw armed guards appear and start patrolling the grounds. One walked the perimeter of the fence, whilst another picked his way around the building. A third stood in the main doorway, stamping his feet to stay warm.

Drake and the others waited. Gradually, the surrounding cars disappeared as the local workers finished their shifts, but there were still enough to offer them a decent concealment. Drake checked his watch.

'We go at nine,' he said.

'How can we be sure Soroyan's in there?' Mai asked.

'We have his picture,' Drake said. 'We saw him go in at midday. Haven't seen him emerge yet.'

'And there's no back way out,' Kenzie said. 'I checked.'

'It's a big place,' Mai said.

'You sound like you don't want to hit it,' Alicia said.

'It's not that. We're unprepared. Don't know how many we're up against. I don't want us to fuck this up.'

Drake turned in his seat to face her. 'Do we ever fuck anything up?'

Mai stared at him. 'Are you kidding me? We're world class at it.'

Alicia huffed. Drake expected a harsh comment but saw Alicia hold back. The Englishwoman was sensitive to Mai's pain and didn't want to add to it. Drake was amazed at her restraint. It was completely out of Alicia's character. Still... it wasn't a bad step forward.

Nobody questioned Mai. Drake continued to stare at her. 'Do you want to do this or not?' He gave her the choice.

The ex-Ninja took a deep breath and then nodded. 'We're at the top of our game,' she said. 'Couldn't be a better time to do it.'

Carefully, they equipped themselves with the weapons they'd bought earlier. Drake stowed a battered Glock in his waistband and hefted a scruffy semi-auto in his hands. The others sorted between the other weapons, shaking their heads at the paltry offerings.

'One thing I miss about working for the US government,' Dahl muttered. 'They always supplied the best of weapons to us.'

'You sound spoiled,' Drake said.

'I enjoy being spoiled,' Dahl hit back. 'I deserve it.'

'I'm a Yorkshireman,' Drake told him. 'We don't do spoiled.'

'No? But I've heard you do whippets.'

Drake shook his head, refusing to get drawn into a slanging match. He checked the time. 'Check,' he said. 'We move in fifteen.'

They counted down the seconds. Made themselves ready. Soon, they opened their doors together and were sneaking out into the night. They stayed low, passing through the parking area between cars. They held their weapons lightly, ready to act. Drake led the way, flitting from car to car until he reached the road.

He crouched, peering across.

The fence was clear, the guard somewhere on the other side of the compound. The building was clear too, its guard around the other side. It was the perfect time to go. The only problem was the guard at the door. He looked bored and was smoking a cigarette, but stood in shadow. Drake couldn't tell which way he was looking.

'We go around,' he said.

They made their way to the right until the door guard was out of sight. Now, the fence guard was approaching, so they stooped down until he'd passed. Then, more bad luck. The building guard appeared on his circuit and they were forced to wait another few minutes until he'd gone.

Finally, the coast was clear.

Drake ran out first, reached the fence, and quickly climbed it, jumping down on the other side. His colleagues did the same and soon they were all crouched inside the compound. Drake saw a huddle of abandoned cars to the right and ran to them. Here, they waited.

The fence guard soon came around again. They

couldn't leave him here in case he raised the alarm. Mai, face set hard, was the first to act. She rose behind the strolling, unsuspecting guard, gripped his larynx, and stopped him from uttering any noise. Then she dragged him backwards, choking the life out of him. The guard fought, dropped his weapon, kicked at her with his heels. But Mai held on grimly, giving him no quarter. Soon, his body went limp, and he slithered to the ground.

Next up, the building guard. They crept forward to a corner and waited for him to come around. When he did, Kinimaka faced him, hammering down with a tree-trunk-like arm right on top of the guy's head. It was instant lights out and then zip ties and a gag. They moved on to the next phase of their plan.

The guard by the door.

First, Dahl dragged the guards' unmoving forms into darkness and shadow so that they'd be less easily seen. Next, the team made their way to another corner from which they could see the front door. Drake peered around. There was about twenty feet between him and the guard – twenty wide open feet.

'It's not a problem,' Dahl said. 'Who's the smallest?'

'Eh?' Drake said.

'It's pretty dark. The building guard was small. We just walk around pretending it's him. Get close to the guard and whack him.'

The men all looked at each other. Cam came forward. 'I guess that's me,' he said.

'Are you good with it?' Dahl asked.

Cam nodded. 'Don't forget – I was trained by Ninjas.'

Drake remembered well when Cam and Shaw had disappeared for a few months helping one of the last surviving Ninja clans in Japan. He stood aside, watched Cam start wandering along the building in a close approximation of how the original guard had walked. Cam neared the door guard. Drake watched carefully, in case he needed to take action. Cam passed the building guard and then lashed out, catching the man at the throat and folding him over. Next, Cam delivered a harsh stomach punch and then a blow to a descending head. The guard hit the ground hard, not moving.

Drake and the others rushed along the side of the building.

They reached the front door, still undetected. They had completed their infiltration of the grounds. Now, they had to get inside.

Drake peered through the door. A lobby stood on the other side, bristling with cardboard boxes. They pushed their way inside, enjoying the warmth. Immediately, they lost themselves among the boxes as a man and woman walked through. Luckily, the pair grabbed a couple of boxes and then just departed, heading deeper into the building.

Drake looked at the other, wishing they had some kind of Bluetooth earbud communication device. They made things so much safer. But they were here on a shoestring, and completely off the books. This was all for Connor Bryant.

They started exploring the lobby, confident it was otherwise empty. Drake checked a back room, found filing cabinets and a large desk and a couple of chairs. More cardboard boxes sat on the table. He exited, found the others, looked deeper into the building.

'On me,' he said.

They penetrated the building further. First, they followed a long, straight corridor, creeping slowly. When someone entered from the far end, they ducked into an office, crouching in the darkness as the man passed them by. Seconds later, they were swiftly up again, emerging back out into the corridor.

They searched quietly and quickly. They found a man in the last office, his attention on the papers spread in front of him. Before he could raise the alarm, Kenzie vaulted his desk and delivered a two-footed kick to his face. The man went down like a sack of spanners, unconscious before he even fell out of his seat.

They tied him up and moved on.

The straight corridor led to an open warehouse where, perhaps, cars had once been stored, maybe even displayed. There were still a few old relics scattered around, rusting gradually, seizing up, and a few oil drums, boxes, and even several sturdy looking crates. Whatever business Soroyan conducted out of here, it clearly needed a lot of storage.

Drake crept across the open space, eyes on a swivel. He felt hugely exposed and conspicuous, but there was no other way through. As he approached the very last car in the wide space, his luck ran out.

Ahead, two men came out of the door they'd been aiming for.

The men stopped and blinked as soon as they saw the invaders. Their faces registered shock. Drake started running immediately, preferring that to shooting as the noise would give the game away. Unfortunately, the two men were armed.

They pulled handguns from around their hips. Drake and the others rolled behind the nearby cars. Gunfire rang out, echoing around the large space. Drake cursed. Now the game was well and truly up. He peered around the side of the car, offered the two men a short burst of his semi-auto.

It scattered them, sent them diving for cover behind an old crate. Drake could only imagine what mayhem had just started up throughout the dealership. Soon, they'd be inundated with opponents.

They still had to do this quick. Drake fired a covering salvo as Dahl and Kinimaka ran to the crates and put their backs to the blind side. When one man peered out, Kinimaka was in his face, grabbed an arm and pulled him out of cover. When he was in space, Kinimaka shot him with his handgun. The other shooter was also unlucky. Dahl had crept around the other side of the crate and came up behind him. A blow to the head rendered him unconscious.

'Clear,' the big Swede yelled.

Drake and the others ran out into the open. They sprinted for the far door, Dahl and Kinimaka now back with them. They reached the door and flung it open, peered into the corridor beyond.

It was empty for now.

Taking advantage, the Ghost Squadron raced into the corridor and checked the rooms to either side. They knew they were again riding their luck. Twenty seconds later, that luck ran out.

The far door opened and several armed men stepped through.

Drake and the others were suddenly exposed, in the open. They fell to their knees and opened fire.

CHAPTER NINE

Bullets laced the air.

Drake dived at a partially open door, hit it hard, and rolled through the opening. A bullet slammed into the wood a few inches from his heels. He rose quickly to a crouch, aimed his gun around the corner, and opened fire. For a moment, the attacking salvo paused, and a man cried out in pain.

He looked into the corridor. Ahead, a group of men were standing, guns raised. They hadn't taken cover. One of them was lying on the ground, groaning. To Drake's left, his team was partially visible, most of them having rolled into the room across the corridor.

Ahead, the group of men kept coming. Drake fired into their midst. That finally made them scatter, and another man went down, this one clutching his gut.

Drake stayed in the open, waiting. On seeing a head pop itself around a corner, he fired. The bullet missed, but the man cried out and dropped his gun. On the other side of the corridor, Dahl was leaning out, trying a different angle.

There was random gunfire up and down the corridor. Drake didn't believe he was pinned down. They simply had to keep moving forward. Soroyan was inside this building and, probably, not far away.

He was also probably feeling pretty superior, even under attack. He would have his defences in place.

But he'd never come up against the Ghost Squadron.

Drake leaned out, fired another shot. He changed mags quickly. A man showed his bulk, angling for a shot. Drake put a bullet in his shoulder, made him fall out into the open. Drake then finished him. He glanced across the corridor at Dahl.

'Corridor's wide enough for three of us,' the Swede said.

Drake knew exactly what he meant. 'Distance is short,' he said. 'We can pull it off.'

Alicia was also listening in to the conversation. 'I'm up for it,' she said.

Drake readied his weapon. He took a deep breath. Then, both he and Dahl leaned out into the corridor and started firing, laying down their own cover. A second later, they rose and stepped out, Alicia in the middle of them. They walked quickly and fired constantly, giving their enemy no chance of returning fire. They raced down the corridor in seconds, reaching their enemy's hiding places and then attacking them.

Drake saw two men, crouching, their backs to the wall, waiting for the endless salvo to stop. They looked up at him, surprise in their eyes.

Quickly, he shot them.

On the other side of the corridor, Dahl finished off two other men. Alicia arrived too late and looked slightly aggrieved.

'All that risk,' she said. 'And I didn't even get a chance to shoot someone.'

Drake looked at her. 'Well, don't get any ideas. I'm not bulletproof.'

They had no time to waste. Drake waited a few seconds for the rest of their team to arrive, then went through the door.

They entered another wide space. They went quickly, ducking low, knowing their presence had been well and truly announced. It was a good job. There were two men on the other side, both with guns raised. Drake dived headlong, and so did Dahl. Alicia started firing instantly, not missing a beat. It was her salvo that took out the two men before they'd even got a shot off.

'Happy now?' Drake said.

The Englishwoman shrugged. They were inside a storage area. A large door stood at the other end, offering them only one way through. It wasn't exactly surprising when that door burst open and three men came running through. It *was* surprising when Drake then saw a fourth man swagger through.

Soroyan.

Even now, clad in his supreme criminal kingpin arrogance, certain he couldn't be beaten. He could see his own dead men, but offered them a supercilious sneer.

'You will die for what you have done today,' he said.

Drake wondered whether they should just open fire, kill the lot of them, but he wanted to get closer. He signalled the team, and they all started creeping across the space, closing in on Soroyan.

'Who are you?' Soroyan asked, confident behind his armed guard.

It was Mai who answered. 'Us?' she said. 'We're the angels of vengeance.'

'I have wronged you in some way? Well, that's hardly surprising. I upset many people and don't lose a moment's sleep over it.'

'Upset?' Mai repeated. 'You fucking murder people.' And she raised her weapon.

Drake glanced at her. 'Think about what you're doing,' he said.

'It's hardly in cold blood,' Alicia said. 'We're in the middle of a bloody firefight here.'

Mai's gun hand wavered.

Soroyan's guards were pointing their guns at her. They seemed to be waiting for an order from their boss.

Soroyan regarded her calmly. 'Did I hurt someone you care about?' His face was expressionless.

Mai swallowed heavily. She licked her lips. Her finger tightened on the trigger. 'You absolute-'

She never finished. One guard, beyond himself, fired first. The bullet winged itself across the space, flashing a few millimetres past Mai's right ear.

Drake started sprinting, gun up, shooting as he went. The others did the same. Soroyan dropped to the floor, looking surprised. His guards were hit, two of them going down instantly. The third fell to his knees and started firing back. Drake and the others ducked into cover.

Soroyan was still scrabbling on the floor. His guard fired a constant stream of bullets until his gun ran dry, keeping Drake and the team sheltering. Drake counted the bullets. He knew just when the gun would empty.

When it did, he ducked back out, lined up the guard and fired. The guard somehow ducked out of the way, the bullet going astray. Soroyan was behind him, lying flat out.

The guard ran. He threw his gun away and raced for the door, waving his arms. Drake was momentarily nonplussed, as were the rest of his team, and they didn't put a bullet in his back. The guard disappeared at a rapid rate.

Soroyan, suddenly alone, scrabbled for the discarded gun. He grabbed it, raised it, and started shooting at them as they came out of hiding, the hammer falling on empty chambers. The dry clicks were like death knells in the air.

The team approached. Soroyan was on his knees. Soon he rose and threw the gun at them. It bounced off Dahl's chest and clattered to the floor. Drake glanced quickly around, put Cam and Shaw on guard duty. They would protect their backs.

Soroyan faced them alone, his back to the door. The only good thing Drake could say about him was that he hadn't tried to run. At least he wasn't a complete coward.

And then Soroyan eyed the door at his back, gathered himself.

Mai fired her gun. Soroyan almost leapt out of his skin. The bullet struck the ground between his legs.

'You're going nowhere except to hell,' she said.

She lined him up in her sights.

'I don't want to die,' Soroyan said quietly.

'Neither did my boyfriend. Neither did the others at Glacier. They were worth a thousand of you.'

'This is about Glacier?' Soroyan looked surprised.

'They stole something from me.'

'You should never have messed with Glacier,' Mai said. 'With us.'

There was an extended silence. Soroyan's mouth was tight, his face white. He looked to be struggling with himself, as if forcing himself not to start begging for his life. In the end, he lost. He flung out his arms and fell to his knees.

'Please don't,' he said. 'I'm sorry for what I did.'

'I just wish I had a knife,' Mai said. 'Because this is personal.'

'I am a man of means. I could give you anything. I just want to be left alone. To survive. Please.'

Mai gritted her teeth.

'I'll do it for you, Mai,' Alicia suddenly said, raising her weapon.

And Drake saw compassion in her face. He knew Alicia was offering to take the burden from Mai because she knew all about the heavy load it would impart on her soul.

'This is cold blood,' Hayden said quietly. 'It's not a firefight anymore.'

Mai looked at her. 'You're saying this fucker should be left alive?'

'It's not like we can take him to the cops,' Shaw said. 'Or get him locked up. If we leave him here now, he'll just carry on with his old ways.'

Soroyan let out a half sob. Drake peered at him more closely, wondering if he was faking. The man's eyes were rock hard.

'Fuck him,' Mai said and pulled the trigger.

CHAPTER TEN

The bullet flashed past Soroyan's left ear.

The man wobbled, legs turning to jelly. He practically fell to the floor and then let out a long gasp. His mouth opened and closed ineffectually.

'Get on your feet,' Mai hissed.

But Soroyan couldn't stand. Drake decided he wasn't putting on an act. Soroyan could barely keep from grovelling on the floor. He managed to raise himself to his knees, hands up.

'Please,' he said. 'Oh, please, don't shoot me.'

'We came a long way to shoot you,' Mai told him. 'You sit here in your rotten kingdom, handing out kill orders, lording it over everyone and everything, happy in your depravity. You affect lives every day, not caring who you hurt, who you destroy. One lost life can devastate dozens of people. And you think you deserve to live?'

The gun wavered again in her hand. Her finger on the trigger was white.

'It will haunt you forever,' Hayden said. 'Killing him this way will haunt you forever.'

'I came here to kill him,' Mai said.

'It's pure cold vengeance,' Kinimaka said.

Mai bit her lip until Drake saw the blood flow. He didn't want her to kill Soroyan in cold blood purely because of the burden it would leave on her, but was torn. Soroyan deserved to die. It would have been better if he'd died in the battle.

Mai flicked her gaze across to Hayden and Kinimaka. 'You're telling me you wouldn't do the same if it was one of you avenging the other?'

Their faces fell. Kinimaka opened his mouth to say something and then closed it quickly. Hayden let out a pensive breath.

Soroyan shook on his knees. 'If you don't kill me, I can help you,' he whispered.

Mai barely heard him. Drake saw her struggling and said, 'You'd say anything to save yourself, you piece of shit.'

And then he turned to Mai. 'Think about it, love.'

His thick Yorkshire accent always came out in times of great stress. Drake felt desperate to help his friend.

Mai walked forward, held the gun close to Soroyan's head. 'This is for Connor.'

'No! Wait! I can help you. I told you I can help. Don't kill me. I will tell you everything.'

Mai hesitated, a millisecond from putting a bullet in his brain.

Drake and Hayden both stepped forward at the same time, hoping to defuse the situation, to pacify Mai. 'What are you talking about?'

'I have knowledge,' Soroyan said. 'I have terrible knowledge.'

Drake shook his head but eased a little sigh of relief when he saw Mai relax slightly. 'You gonna try to get rid of your competitors, Soroyan?'

It was an old trick of criminals. Giving

information about their rivals so they'd rid themselves of the competition. Something a man like Soroyan would love to do.

'Nothing like that,' Soroyan said. 'The information I have will change the world.'

'The world?' Drake repeated, slightly taken aback. What could Soroyan possibly know...

'Don't kill me,' Soroyan repeated, tears leaking from the corner of his eyes. 'Promise me.' He looked up at Mai.

She smashed the gun into his face, drawing blood from above his right eye. 'Rat bastard,' she growled.

'If I were you,' Drake said. 'I'd spill everything to save your life.'

Soroyan looked at the Yorkshireman as if trying to gauge the worth of his life. At this stage, it wasn't worth a whole lot.

'You understand what I tell you, I am not involved in,' Soroyan said. 'I would never...'

Knowing how terrible Soroyan was, Drake got a bad feeling. 'Just stop with the bullshit and tell us what you know,' he said.

'Someone is planning an attack,' he said. 'A joint attack. They are planning to hit London, New York and Los Angeles with chemical weapons and they already have all the manpower in place.'

Drake watched the man's face as he spoke. Was he lying, trying to con them to save his life? It seemed likely. But if there was just a kernel of truth to his words...

'Details,' Hayden said.

'I don't have any. All I know is that three major cities are going to be targeted soon and the plans are already near fruition.'

'You have to know something else,' Kinimaka said. 'How can we verify it?'

Soroyan close his eyes and Drake saw fear jump into his face. But this was a different fear than he offered to Mai. This was deep-seated terror.

'I know who is organising it,' he said. 'A terrible, legendary terrorist called the Dark Tsar. Have you heard the name?'

'I have,' Dahl said. 'From my days in the special forces. You're right to say legendary. He was more a fable.'

Soroyan nodded. 'Yes, yes, a nightmare whispered around campfires. People say his name and reputation were made up to scare law enforcement.'

'And you're saying this man is *real?*' Hayden asked.

'The Dark Tsar is indeed real,' Soroyan told them. 'As an arms dealer, I have had many dealings with him. It is why I am privy to his plans. I have known the man for decades.'

'So you're loyal then,' Alicia said sarcastically.

'To myself,' Soroyan bit back, a little more confident now that he knew they were listening. 'I don't know what else to say about the Dark Tsar, except that he's a flesh and blood nightmare terrorist that even people like me fear. He's the sort of man who wishes to change the world, to instil fear and violence and blood into everyday life. I have my business, yes, but I stay within certain boundaries. The Dark Tsar just wants chaos.'

'We've come across a few like that,' Alicia said. 'They're all dead.'

'The Dark Tsar is unkillable,' Soroyan said. 'It's part of his legend.'

Drake shifted his feet. 'Tell us more.'

'He's ancient, deadly, skilled in all forms of combat. He's in his forties, smart as a whip, loyal to those who help him. He's thirty-three, deadly, eager to kill even friends who make even the slightest mistake. The man has palaces, underground caves, a castle, a state-of-the-art mansion. Do you see the legend now?'

Drake nodded. 'No one has a fucking clue.'

'It's exactly what he wants. Chaos. He probably cultivates it all, invents new legends every week.'

'But you know him,' Kenzie said. 'You told us.'

'I know a voice on the phone, yes. I have spoken to him, never seen him. He is still a mystery to me.'

'And yet he told you all his plans?' Dahl sounded unconvinced.

Soroyan made a face. 'I won't repeat this, ever. I won't incriminate myself on any record. But I might have supplied certain items required to make this job happen. I was given the addresses in all three cities where the attacks will happen. And, as I said, it will be soon. Everything is in place.'

'He just wants to ruin the world,' Hayden said speculatively.

Soroyan nodded. 'The Dark Tsar is one of the worst. He's clever, crazy, cunning. He's been getting away with far more than me for decades. There isn't a lawful eye on him because three quarters of them don't even believe he's real. Now...' he looked up at them. 'You said you wouldn't kill me.'

Mai, still holding the gun pointed at his head, backed away. Drake could tell she was still uncertain, still torn.

'We may need him,' he said.

'He's not worth a bullet,' Alicia said. 'The scum of the earth.'

Soroyan had become fearful again as he turned to look at Mai. Her expression was terrifying.

'He killed Connor,' she said.

Drake walked forward and slowly held out his hand for the gun. 'Don't ruin yourself, love.'

Mai's glance flicked to him. He saw tears in her eyes. Her frame shook. He shook his head. After a moment, Mai slapped the gun into his hands, turned away, and took a deep breath. Soroyan collapsed in relief.

The team found themselves staring at each other. Now they possessed the same terrible knowledge as Soroyan. The question was – what were they going to do with it?

'What's the next step?' Cam asked. 'Who would listen to us?'

Drake knew that, logically, if the man had still been alive, this would have been passed along to Bryant.

Now...

'There's only one thing to do,' he said. 'We all know the man we should be speaking to.'

CHAPTER ELEVEN

It was a complex and crazy situation. They needed to act fast. What should they do with Soroyan? They couldn't exactly drag him along, and they hated leaving him to get on with his dreadful business. It was a surprising fact that a team that had fought and worked for different agencies for so long, and been highly successful, could think of only one man to take their information too.

Drake led the way out of the dealership. They left Soroyan behind, warning that they'd be back if they heard anything bad about his future business dealings. They knew he'd go right back to his nefarious dealings, but at least they'd tried. In the end, Mai contented herself with knocking him out.

It wasn't what he deserved, but it helped to keep the burden of murder off her conscience.

They raced for the car, started it up, and headed directly for the airport. As Dahl drove, Hayden took out her phone.

'You have his number?' Drake asked. 'I have it here.'

Hayden nodded. 'I've had it programmed into my phone for a long time.'

She made the call, waited for it to go through. It rang and rang. Nobody picked up. In the end, she had to leave a message for the man to call her back. She punched the back of the seat, frustrated. 'Are you kidding me?' she said. 'I'm trying to report the end of the world and all I get is voicemail.'

Dahl drove as fast as he dared, cutting sharply through the traffic. Buildings flashed past to either side. A soft drizzle filled the air, coating the windscreen. It was cold too, prompting Drake to turn up the heating. The sat nav told them they were thirty-two minutes away from the airport. It felt like an age.

At the same time, Kinimaka was searching for the earliest, fastest flight out of the country.

Ten minutes later, Hayden's phone started to ring. She let out a sigh of relief. 'Hi.'

'This is Patrick Sutherland,' the man said. 'Hayden, you said it was life or death?'

Drake listened as Hayden spoke to their contact. The assistant director of the FBI had helped them out numerous times in the past, including a time when they were forced to challenge the President of the United States.

'We're in Budapest, sir, and we've stumbled across some vital information. I won't go into all the details of why we're here, but a criminal by the name of Soroyan – a notorious arms dealer – has bartered for his life by telling us this,' she continued, telling Sutherland all she knew. 'And we have the three addresses.'

Sutherland was silent for a while, taking it all in. Dahl drove them ever closer to the airport and Kinimaka was tapping away on a tablet, booking them on flights.

'How soon can you get back?' Sutherland asked.

Hayden glanced at Kinimaka.

'Fifteen hours until we land,' Kinimaka said.

Hayden passed on the information. Sutherland was quiet for another minute, clearly thinking it all through. 'Give me the addresses,' he said. 'And stay in touch. Let me know when you land and I'll tell you where to go. This will all be coordinated from here, DC, so you're headed for the right place. How reliable is your information?'

Hayden hesitated. 'Too reliable to ignore,' she said at last. 'The arms dealer was in fear of his life.'

Sutherland said nothing to that. The guy could still be lying. But he seemed to take Hayden's words on board. 'Get back as soon as you can,' he said.

The team raced into the airport, dropped off the car and then hurried through check in and customs. They had two hours to wait for their flight, so grabbed a decent meal and sat back with a few drinks. They were on edge, ready to act and fight. It was an odd situation, something they'd never come across before, and it unsettled them. At least, it unsettled Drake. He assumed it was the same for the others.

'You think he's lying?' he asked, sipping a double vodka.

'I think I should have shot him,' Mai grumbled.

'The information saved his life,' Kinimaka said. 'We can't verify it, but he knows we can always go back to finish him if it's a load of bull. The way he acted... the way he responded... I'd say it's all true.'

The others all nodded. Everyone seemed in agreement. Drake sat back and tried to relax. This long wait was going to be interminable, but it would at least give Sutherland the chance to get the ball rolling. The hours and minutes dragged past. Their flight was called. They boarded, sat down, waited for it to take off. Soon, they were in the air, the plane engines roaring steadily through the clouds.

Drake knew he should take a nap. He tried unsuccessfully. It wasn't the journey; it was what was going on inside his head. If this Dark Tsar succeeded with his attacks, the world would indeed change. And if he *did* succeed, what was to stop him from carrying out worse attacks? Success would only embolden him, and hundreds like him.

The plane chased the light all across the sky. By the time they came within sight of Washington, DC, it was early afternoon of the following day. Drake could see a network of roads spread out below as the plane banked.

Then it had landed, and they were through the checks and outside the airport. Hayden immediately called Sutherland.

'We're at the airport.'

He reeled off an address. 'Meet me here immediately.'

It was nonstop. They jumped into a cab, gave out the address, and relaxed. Drake felt as if they were racing ahead at the same time as sitting back. It was an odd sensation.

The cab cut through the heavy DC traffic, taking a few side streets to ease the strain. Soon, they were pulling up outside their building.

Drake saw a bland office block with opaque windows and a barred front door. He made his way over, pressed a buzzer, and announced himself. Soon, an armed guard came to the door and opened it up, beckoned them all through. Drake found himself inside an open plan office area. They followed the guard and his leather shoulder holster all the way through. Drake noticed the man's gun was huge and turned when Alicia nudged him.

'I wonder if he's compens-'
'Don't finish that sentence.'
'Why not?'
'It could get us shot.'

They passed through the room, stopping at a far door. Here, the guard paused and then opened it fully. A wave of noise rushed in. Drake saw a large conference room packed with people and then pushed his way in. There was a briefing going on. Patrick Sutherland hadn't waited for them, but he had given them every chance to attend.

Sutherland was standing on a makeshift podium at the far end of the room, shouting so that everyone could hear him. Drake counted at least fifty people in the windowless room.

'We're covering three different addresses in three different cities,' Sutherland was saying. 'We're going to hit them all at the same time so that they can't react to the attack and set off a bomb or something in retaliation. The Brits are waiting for us in London. When we land, we go in.'

'Why are they waiting for us?' someone asked.

'They're not convinced by the information.' Sutherland shrugged. 'They're reacting too slowly. They'll help, but say it's our operation and we should have operatives on site. I don't blame them. There's been no chatter about this.'

'Can't we send in local operatives?' someone else asked.

'We want the right operatives,' Sutherland said. 'I have a team in mind.'

'What are the locations?' a voice asked.

Sutherland consulted his notes. 'In London, it's a dockland warehouse. In New York, it's a residential address. In Los Angeles, it's a Hollywood Hills villa.'

'They're the targets?' Someone said. 'They don't sound very prestigious.'

Sutherland raised an eyebrow. 'No. They're the addresses where the teams behind the bombings are working out of. Our friendly arms dealer delivered to these places. He has no idea what the targets are.'

'Let's hope the bombs aren't in place yet,' a woman said.

'All the reason to move fast,' Sutherland said. 'Now, you have your information. That's it. Time to get to work.'

The meeting broke up, droves of people heading for the door. Drake and the others stood aside and gradually made their way to Sutherland's side.

'Ah, you're here,' he said, spying them. 'You've certainly started a massive operation this time. God knows, I hope you're right.'

'So do we,' Drake said. 'Especially with those addresses.'

Sutherland nodded. 'I want you at every address,' he said. 'Go with the teams now. They're already headed out.'

Drake turned to the others. Hayden was already assessing them. 'So who's headed where?' she said.

CHAPTER TWELVE

Drake and Dahl chose London. They arrived to a heavy sleet, a blanket of fog, and headed out to meet the team already on the ground. This team comprised ten SAS soldiers, a sight which sent long-forgotten thoughts spinning around Drake's head. It had been many years since he'd rolled with the SAS, but he had endless fond memories. In the intermediate years, he hadn't thought about the outfit much. He'd just been getting on with life. But to run into a living, breathing unit – it took him back, brought him up short for a while.

The commander came forward and introduced himself. 'Brady,' he said gruffly. 'I lead this team. Are you guys ready?'

Drake nodded. 'Drake and Dahl,' he said. 'At your service.'

'Then let's get going.'

They all piled into a large van, most of them sitting on benches in the back. Their weapons were inside. Drake and Dahl were given HK MP5 submachine guns and Glock 17s. They were also supplied black tactical vests and impeccable comms gear, which they slotted into their ears. The driver of the van shouted out a ten-minute warning.

It was all happening insanely fast. Drake felt like

his feet had barely touched the ground and here they were, about to arrive at their destination. Of course, they wouldn't start the assault yet. That would be coordinated simultaneously across all three cities.

The van drove carefully at the speed limit. It entered the docklands and made its way more steadily, approaching its destination. When close, it parked up and switched off, its occupants now sitting in the suddenly quiet interior.

Brady checked his comms. 'Waiting on your go.'

Drake sat in silence, the hulking figure of Dahl at his side. Drake let his eyes drift across the faces of the SAS guys. These visages, these expressions – they were the same as in his day. Severe, highly trained men and women gearing up for a fight, their minds fully focused on the job. It felt a little surreal working with them once again.

How long had it been? He couldn't even remember and didn't want to think about it too hard.

Dahl leaned in to him. 'You think Soroyan was telling the truth?'

Drake shrugged. 'I do. I think he knew Mai was really going to kill him at one point.'

'Better for her that she didn't,' Dahl said. 'She'll heal faster.'

Drake thought about Bryant, about what had happened at Glacier. All because a politician's daughter got kidnapped and then rescued.

'What do you know about this Dark Tsar?' he asked.

Dahl shifted slightly. 'Very little beyond what you already know. Half my team and the office analysts didn't believe he existed. They thought he was just another terrorist crew, blowing in the wind. He was the enemy you could attribute anything to. If you didn't know who committed an atrocity, you went with the Dark Tsar. That kind of thing.'

'Maybe it was,' Drake said.

Dahl shrugged. 'Maybe.'

Brady spoke up from the front. 'Hang tight. Just synchronising the three attacks. We're almost there.'

Drake knew Brady wouldn't have spoken unless they were practically ready to move. He readied himself, rolled his shoulders, prepared mentally.

Brady raised a fist, then brought it down. A soldier opened the rear doors and jumped out. Soon, they were all outside, their guns raised and ready. Brady was the last to exit the van and fling the door closed behind him.

Ahead stood a warehouse. It looked rundown. There were three windows across its front, all cracked, with walls consisting of flaking paint. The place looked deserted and was surrounded by other functioning sites. Brady pointed to the door and said, 'Move out.'

The team raced for the front door. As they did so, one of the windows shattered. There came the sound of a gunshot. They'd been seen. Drake ducked, but the bullet had already flown by. The rest of the team went to ground.

More gunshots sounded. The other windows broke. Glass rained down. Two SAS soldiers were already at the door and now kicked it in before ducking down to take cover. Bullets slammed through the new opening.

Drake crawled across the tarmac, face close to the

ground. He took cover behind a rusty old skip, hearing bullets clanging off the yellowish metal. When he glanced out from cover, he couldn't see into the building, couldn't make out his enemy.

They had to get closer.

It wouldn't be difficult for the SAS. Soldiers were inching closer all the time, communicating with each other through their earbuds. Drake got a constant trickle of information and now heard what they were going to do next.

Stun grenades.

Four men rose swiftly and flung the grenades high, angling them through the broken windows. The grenades flew through the air, tumbling inside the building. The guns instantly stopped chattering. A moment later there were four dull thuds. Instantly, the SAS team was on its feet and out of cover, rushing towards the doorway.

They slipped inside. Drake saw wooden tables and a mass of machinery, benches all along the sides, and heaps of boxes in one corner. There were six men that he could see, all with their hands clapped to their ears, all struggling to stay upright and keep hold of their weapons. As the SAS team appeared, they tried to recover and fire. Errant bullets flew in all directions.

Faced with that chaos, Drake again fell to the floor. Bullets were slamming into walls, into the ceiling, stitching holes into the floor as the terrorists struggled to find their equilibrium. An SAS soldier was unluckily tagged, a bullet catching him in the arm.

The team sliced into the building like a hot knife

through butter. All that held them up was the chaos. The terrorists staggered and fired, some of them now clear-headed enough to take cover.

Drake saw two of them go down before that happened. They spun in the air, taken out by the SAS. Drake scrambled forward steadily, moving between table legs and bypassing boxes. Dahl was a few paces behind him.

'If possible,' Brady said in his ear. 'Try to take a few of them alive.'

Drake rose, saw a terrorist in a green T-shirt, fired a round at his upper mass. He tagged the man's shoulder, sent him spinning. He ran forward. Another terrorist popped his head up from cover and raised his weapon, but Dahl fired first, bullets exploding all around the man and sending him back into cover.

Drake reached the man he'd injured and smashed him across the face with his gun. The man was solid. He barely moved. Drake knew he couldn't just stand there and fight. He was too easy a target. He dropped before the man, punched him in the groin. The terrorist folded and fought to position his gun so that it pointed at Drake.

Drake grabbed it, punched the man in the face. Again, he didn't budge. All around them, gunmen were firing their weapons and trying to shake off the aftereffects of the stun grenades. The SAS were among them. There was shooting and fighting, a great melee among the machinery and the boxes.

Drake slung his weapon across his shoulder so that he had both hands free. He grabbed the barrel of the other man's gun, forced it down to the floor. He punched his opponent in his injured shoulder. This finally caused a reaction, making the other man groan. Drake then smashed him across the face. Blood flew from a broken nose and teeth. The man continued to fight, though, as tough as any opponent Drake had faced before.

Suddenly, Dahl was in the fracas. He took one look at the terrorist, raised a huge fist and brought it slamming down on top of the man's head. Instantly, he slumped and slithered to the floor, unconscious.

'Why were you playing with him?' Dahl asked smugly.

Drake panted and shook his head. 'Bell end.'

'But useful.'

Drake looked ahead. There was another terrorist well-hidden behind a row of oil drums, his gun resting on top. The moment he saw anything move, he fired. Drake ducked as he became the target.

Bullets clanged all around, striking machinery. Drake crawled forward, approaching the hidden terrorist. He came from low level, out of the man's eyeline, came right up to the oil drums.

The gun was balanced above him.

He reached up, grabbed the barrel, and pulled. There was a gasp of shock and then a swift movement. Drake yanked the gun away, flung it down, and then Dahl was vaulting over the oil drums and kicking their opponent in the face. The man went down instantly, without putting up a fight.

Most of the SAS were engaged in close combat now. Drake could see two terrorists slumped across a couple of benches who wouldn't be talking. He knew at least one more had been killed in the firefight. He reached down to haul up the man Dahl had knocked out. The SAS had picked up only one casualty – the man who'd been shot in the shoulder.

Drake handed the man to Dahl and then continued his way through the warehouse, alert for anyone who might be hiding. Two other soldiers were doing the same. In the end, they came to the far wall without coming across another enemy.

Job done, Drake thought.

The soldiers began interrogating the living terrorists. Soon, they would know where the chemical weapon was and whether it had been planted yet. And Drake had no doubt the terrorists would spill all they knew. This wasn't playtime. This was the big leagues, with thousands of lives on the line. Soon, the threat would be neutralised. His mind then went instantly to the rest of his team.

Dahl came up on the right. 'I hope they're okay,' he said.

Drake decided not to tell him he'd been thinking along the same lines. Instead, he pointed at the man held in Dahl's right hand.

'Shall we get started?'

'Yeah. I hope the bastard tries to hold out on us.'

Drake shook his head and carefully slapped the man awake. The eyes fluttered, confused at first and then filled with hatred as he remembered where he was.

'Ay up,' Drake said. 'Ready to spill the beans?'

The guy actually looked confused.

'What my fish and chip eating, whippet shagging friend here is trying to say is tell us everything you know,' Dahl said. 'Or we will start to hurt you.'

The Dark Tsar

The terrorist just snarled at them, making the Swede smile. This reaction just made the terrorist's eyes glaze with fright.

Dahl took out his knife.

CHAPTER THIRTEEN

In New York and Manhattan, Alicia, Kenzie, Hayden and Kinimaka were first driven to a staging area in the bowels of an old hotel on Riverside Drive and then transported in several old vans to West 96th Street where their target residence lay. They were given weapons and gear and outfitted with comms devices. They joined a special SWAT team, several in fact, all working together.

Alicia tried to focus. It had been a whirlwind few days. Since Bryant was murdered, everything had changed. The team had barely put a foot on the ground before being whisked off somewhere else. They'd found and almost killed a notorious arms dealer, then let him go. They'd tracked terrorists planning to use chemical weapons in three major cities. And now, they were about to teach those terrorists a harsh lesson.

The residence in question was a four-storey apartment building halfway along the street with the terrorists living on the top floor. The teams were all whisked quickly to the street in unmarked vans and then given a few minutes to prepare. Alicia watched the team leader. He was busy on the phone, coordinating with the other teams.

'Five minutes,' he said. 'Then we all go in sync.'

Alicia hefted her weapon, checked her spare mags. She couldn't see out of the van, so did not know what to expect. All she knew was they had four flights of stairs to run up and then a bunch of terrorists to hit as hard and fast as they could.

Alicia realised she was sitting next to Kenzie, and that she'd let the last ten minutes pass without ribbing the other woman. She hardly ever let a chance like that pass and wondered why. Of course, she knew the reason without thinking. Bryant's death had shocked them all, leeched the sense of fun out of everything. She felt morose, pessimistic. Even the thought of bouncing the heads of a bunch of terrorists barely perked her up. For her part, Kenzie also hadn't tried to tease Alicia. The woman sat staring straight forward, a faraway look in her eyes.

The call came in. Alicia, Kenzie, Hayden, and Kinimaka were in the middle of the SWAT team. The doors opened, and they all jumped out into a bright, blustery day. Alicia saw a typical New York street lined with buildings and with cars parked on both sides. People ambled up and down the pavement, some turning to stare at the SWAT teams.

They acted quickly. As a unit, they ran across the street, pounded up the steps, and breached the front door. They raced for the staircase to the left of the tiny elevator and started up, eighteen men and women, all with their weapons ready and their helmets on. Even Alicia wore her helmet, trying to fit in with the local crews.

The teams rushed up the first flight. A resident exited her room, came face to face with the cops, and almost screamed. A man put his finger to his lips and ushered her back inside her apartment. The woman slammed the door hard. They hastened up another floor. A man was on his way down and they urged him past them faster. Another door opened. An older man put his head out, eyes widening at seeing the activity.

They raced up to the third floor, gear bouncing on their waists. Now, at the top, they slowed. The team leader jumped on the comms.

'Steady pace. Room 408. Hit it hard, but we want to take them alive. Go.'

Alicia patiently waited her turn. She couldn't see how eighteen SWAT cops were going to all assault a small New York apartment, so assumed just the lead few would go in first, with the rest as back up. Those in front were already approaching room 408.

There was a lull as everyone got into position. The team leader was at the head of the pack. He raised a hand, then brought it down fast, slicing the air apart.

A man kicked hard at the door. There was a crash and the sight of it flying inwards. Alicia and the others moved forward as six SWAT officers poured through the door, shouting at the tops of their voices. Almost immediately, there came the sound of gunshots.

Bullets flew through the open door, pounding into the walls. A SWAT officer cried out and fell backwards through the door. Two more took his place. Alicia bit her lip in frustration, wanting to be part of the action. Hayden and Kinimaka were up in front of her, getting closer to the room.

More noise, more gunshots. The sound of people crying out, getting shot, rebounding off furniture.

The wounded officer was dragged away to safety and someone started tending to him. Alicia just wanted to push past everyone and get into the room.

The action went on for long minutes. Another SWAT officer staggered out of the room, clutching his arm. Another took his place, rushing in low. Alicia was unsighted, standing by just in case. Finally, Kinimaka reached the door.

And then the noises stopped. A voice came through the comms.

'Mission success. All the bad guys are down. Two are still alive and in custody.'

There was a cheer along the hallway. SWAT officers started piling into the room, and Alicia went with them, Kenzie at her back. Inside, it was utter chaos. Bullets had riddled the walls and all the furniture. A TV looked like it had exploded. There were four bodies slumped on the floor and two men standing in a far corner, their hands cuffed behind them. Blood had painted the left-hand wall and weapons lay everywhere. The terrorists had been well armed and happy to defend themselves to the death.

The team leader nodded at two of his men. 'Find out what these bastards have done with the chemical weapons,' he said. 'Any way you can.'

CHAPTER FOURTEEN

In Los Angeles, Mai, Cam and Shaw followed a similar pattern to the others, only their journey took them winding up into the Hollywood hills. It was a bright, sunny morning in LA. Not that Mai got to see all that much of it.

They were briefed in a wide, airy, dusty room and then bundled into vans for the long drive into the hills. There was no anxiety about the time. They knew they had plenty and didn't want to arrive too early and stand out like sore thumbs. Mai was seated with Cam and Shaw at her side, the three of them lost in their own thoughts.

For Mai, it wasn't a welcome place to be. Memories floated through her brain as if taunting her, as if they were trying to constantly remind her of everything she'd lost. Bryant wasn't coming back. She would never speak to him again, never see his smile, never rib him about the messy state of his wardrobe at home. How could she deal with that? So far, it had been non-stop action, always moving, always concentrating on something. The hardest part was when she'd been trying to sleep, so she stopped doing that. She was running on fumes, but she was still running. Running hard.

Her friends helped.

The van rocked and swayed on its journey. Mai rocked with it. She tried to focus on the job at hand, on anything else. They were headed up into the Hollywood hills to take out some terrorists. *That should be the focus of all her attentions.*

Eventually, they arrived at their destination and parked up. They were forced to park a few minutes away from their target, as they didn't want to draw any attention to themselves. Now it was time to wait. Wait for the other two teams in London and New York to say they were ready to go.

'We're assaulting a villa,' the team leader told them. 'So it's all hands on deck. We're assuming there's at least six terrorists and any of them could have their fingers on a trigger, so don't take any chances. Sweep the house, try to take some of them alive. Got it?'

There were several nods. Mai knew the routine. She wore a bullet-proof vest and carried a Hechler and Koch, a Glock and a knife. She had two grenades strapped to her belt. Cam and Shaw were similarly attired. Cam leaned in to her now.

'We stop these bastards and we end the threat, yes?'

'A threat we didn't even know about until recently,' Shaw added.

It worried Mai that they hadn't known the intentions of this Dark Tsar. It spoke of a highly motivated, highly capable individual who could carry out practically any attack that he wanted. It spoke of a man someone needed to take down. But it wouldn't be them. In fact, with Bryant dead, she did not know what the future held for the Ghost Squadron.

Perhaps they could branch out with their own firm after all. Hayden had been seriously looking into the idea for a while now.

They waited. The inside of the van was tense. Sweat stood out on several brows. Nobody spoke – everyone already with their game faces on. Mai checked her weapon, something she'd already done twice. The minutes ticked past slowly.

At last, the team leader called out that they were a go. The driver started up the van and set off at speed; the tyres slewing across the gravel. Mai held on tightly as the vehicle bounced and jolted itself for another three minutes.

'Brace!' someone shouted.

And then they hit a gate, the bull bar on the front of this van purposely taking the impact and doing the job. Mai felt the vehicle sway around a short driveway and then come to an abrupt stop, skidding slightly. Again she heard gravel spewing out from beneath the tyres.

No more words were needed. They flung open the back doors along with two other vans and jumped out. Outside, Cam and Shaw were separated into another team. Mai saw a sprawling house, two storeys, with white pillars, a big glass frontage and marble steps. If they were good at their jobs, the terrorists would already know they were under assault. She expected a proactive strike from them, something to give them an advantage, but nothing happened.

Mai raced towards the front door.

She made her way up the front steps, fourth in line. They breached the door hard and entered the house at pace, three teams hitting from three different directions. Mai found herself in a wide hallway with an elaborate staircase to the left, a long corridor to the right, and several doors.

From one door stepped a bearded man. Out of the corner of her eye, from his shape, she knew he was carrying a gun. Mai bent low and swivelled, already firing.

Her bullets struck true, catching the man at the waist before he could get off a shot. The man twisted and fell in the doorway as his blood painted the walls.

They ran for the stairs. At the landing they split up, half the team going left, the other half going right. Mai went right. A terrorist popped his head out of a door ahead, fired immediately. Hot lead sprayed down the hallway, smashing into walls and doorframes. Splinters of wood flew everywhere, one of them puncturing into Mai's calf and making her grunt in pain. The terrorist's shots were returned tenfold, making him duck back out of sight.

Mai kept going, ignoring the pain in her calf. It wasn't too bad. She sighted on the door where the terrorist was hidden, ready to duck and hide at a moment's notice. She saw movement ahead. The terrorist's head reappeared. She fired, bullets destroying the doorframe to the left of his head. There was a scream, but he didn't vanish. Just brought his own gun up and started firing.

A cop fell, hand to his bulletproof vest. Two more went diving to the ground. Mai fell to her knees, firing again. Someone's bullets tore into the terrorist and he cried out, falling through the door into the corridor. He twitched, still alive but dying fast.

Mai ran up to him, kicked his gun away. Now she could hear gunfire coming from elsewhere in the house. She checked the room for other lurkers, but found it empty. The cops were at her side.

They continued down the hallway, but found nothing more. Still, they could hear gunfire and there came the sound of a stun grenade exploding. Quickly, they cleared the floor and then hurried back downstairs.

Through the comms system, they kept in touch with what was going on.

Team three had breached from the rear, finding two terrorists in the kitchen. These men had been unprepared and had easily been captured alive. One of them was still holding his steaming mug of coffee when they tried to slap the plastic cuffs on. Team two had gone in through the huge conservatory, breaking the glass and entering from the side. They had also found two terrorists, but these two had had full access to their weapons. Team two was still involved in a heavy firefight.

Mai could hear it. Along with her team, she rushed through the house in the general direction of the conservatory. They were aiming to come up behind the terrorists, hoping to flush them out.

Mai heard the sounds of gunfire getting louder. She slowed, now at the head of her team. She stopped at a wide, arched doorway, staying low, and looked inside. Team two had been alerted that they were approaching and ceased fire.

Mai peered around the doorway.

She saw both terrorists hunkered down, well

placed behind several overturned iron tables, surrounded by ammo. They were trying to sight on team two and, when they opened fire, they did so for long seconds, the air shivering at the sound of constant gunfire. There were grins plastered on their faces, as if they were enjoying themselves, as if they were involved in some kind of crazy video game.

Mai knew at a glance that they wouldn't come without getting themselves killed. If she showed herself, asked them to surrender, they'd simply fire on her.

She pulled out her stun grenade and threw it. Then she stepped back, knowing the terrorists would spin and fire. Sure enough, they did, bullets smashing into the wall that protected her. She heard the grenade bouncing, then it spinning, and then came an almighty bang.

Instantly, she peered around the door. The terrorists were sitting with their hands over their heads, screaming, their weapons forgotten. Mai gave the order to proceed. She rushed into the room, straight to the weapons, and kicked them all clear. Cops were all around her, scooping up the weapons and dragging the terrorists to their feet. Cops were also pouring in from the direction of the conservatory – team two.

According to the comms, team three was mopping up, sweeping the house for any other bad guys. Half of team two disappeared to do the same. Mai watched as the terrorists were cuffed and then pushed against a wall, surrounded by armed cops.

The interrogations would begin immediately.

Mai knew they had brought trained interrogators

on the mission, and they now stepped forward. She didn't need to see what came next and turned away, listening to the communications coming through her ear.

Minutes later, someone reported that all three missions had been a resounding success. In London, New York and Los Angeles, the good guys had won the day. The terrorists and their chemical weapons had been well and truly neutralised.

For Mai, it was the end of another successful mission. Once again, they had succeeded. Bryant had been avenged as best he could be. In doing so, they had foiled what would have been a massive attack on the world, something that would never have been forgotten.

Now, she could start the grieving process, safe in the knowledge that she had done her job.

CHAPTER FIFTEEN

In Turkey, it was as black as a demon's heart; the sky bereft of stars and even the moon tonight. If one looked up, you could see only the heart of darkness and could be forgiven for thinking the end of the world had come.

In the castle that stood on the craggy hill the mood was dire. It reflected the black night perfectly, giving the impression that its occupants had drawn the blackness right into them, ingesting it as in some kind of freakish game.

And in the highest tower, the tallest peak, the mood was positively murderous.

The tall man with the thunderous visage, the long hair and the steely, deadly eyes, was nothing but a ghost. A legend. He existed on the fringes of the world, and that was how he liked it. They had nothing over him, couldn't tie him to anything. He was a king, a player, a magician. Nobody could stop him.

But now someone *had*.

The Dark Tsar stood in the corner of a room, his hand against a wall, leaning at an angle. His eyes were focused on the floor. He was holding himself upright, shaking with anger. Eight feet to his right, a balding man stood, tension in his eyes.

'They stopped *all* the attacks?' the Dark Tsar said.

'I'm afraid so. Every team – lost. Every bomb – found. We have nothing.'

The Dark Tsar shuddered. Darkness filled his vision. 'Do you know how long I have been planning this? The resources that went into it?'

'Yes, my friend, I do.'

The tsar ground his teeth together until he felt the blood flow. This didn't happen. He was never thwarted, and certainly not on this scale. He glanced over at his old friend and second-in-command.

'Javier,' he said. 'How did this happen?'

'The information is still coming in. It's all very recent. I believe some of their operations are still ongoing.'

'And who is 'they'?'

Javier shrugged. 'The authorities in London, New York and Los Angeles,' he said. 'We know no more than that.'

'They grabbed *all* the teams?'

'I'm afraid so. Killed some. Captured some. Nobody escaped.'

The tsar took a long, deep breath. This had never happened before. But then, he'd done nothing on this scale before.

'Someone... somewhere... talked,' he said.

Javier nodded in agreement. 'The circle was tight,' he said. 'We should squeeze and see what happens.'

The Dark Tsar didn't answer. It didn't matter how much they squeezed. The operation was still ruined. *His* operation. His baby. He'd been in the planning processes for the best part of a year. It had started out as something to while away the time, to keep him busy. Just a dream. But then, as things fell into place, he had realised that he could make his dream a reality. So he and Javier had really started putting their heads together. This was as much Javier's operation as it was his.

'This doesn't happen to me,' he said.

Javier nodded. 'It is unusual. Maybe it was the size of the operation.'

'No. We can go bigger. We can go much bigger.'

Javier made a satisfied face. 'We now have the personnel, the resources, the contacts. I agree.'

The tsar pulled himself away from the wall and started pacing. 'Who else knows about this?'

'Just you and me.'

'Keep it that way as long as you can. This is a failure. It will undermine me, undermine all of us. The three operations should have gone off without a hitch.'

'It won't affect our other operations.'

The tsar thought about the drugs, the prostitution rackets, the various other schemes he had going on. He was far removed from all of them, a ghost. The closest he ever came to being visible was when he strong-armed a powerful politician. That man or woman at least heard his voice.

'I don't know what to do,' he admitted, something he'd never do in front of anyone except Javier. 'I really don't know what to do.'

'We could start again.'

'The same operation? No.' The tsar sighed and walked over to his desk, perching himself on the end. Then he thought better of it and went over to the bar and poured himself a stiff drink. He didn't offer one to Javier, knowing the man was a recovering alcoholic. Instead, he downed it in one and then poured another. He savoured the burn and waited for the welcome numbness.

But he was shaking in anger, in loss, in defeat. He found he couldn't meet Javier's eyes, not with any confidence. He wasn't used to the feeling of defeat and he sure as hell didn't enjoy it.

'Damn,' he said, slamming his glass down. *'Damn!'*

Javier walked closer. 'Move on,' he said. 'That's all we can do. Nobody beyond the circle knows who was behind the attacks.'

'But someone in the circle blabbed,' the tsar snapped. 'This is my defeat. My thrashing. The bastards beat me.'

'And they're probably feeling pretty good about it,' Javier speculated.

The tsar hadn't thought too much about that. Now he considered it and bared his teeth. 'You are right.'

'Maybe we should just join the party below,' Javier said gloomily. 'Cheer ourselves up a bit with a couple of hookers.'

The tsar licked his lips. 'Normally, I'd say good call. But I am having another idea. Another thought.'

'You are?'

'They shouldn't be allowed to get away with this.'

Javier looked confused. 'I already said that. We will find out who talked.'

'I don't mean that bastard. I mean the other bastards. The ones who thwarted us. The authorities... the cops... the special forces. We should make them pay.'

Javier now looked surprised. 'You want to go after the authorities?'

The tsar shook his head. 'No,' he said. 'Not exactly. They ruined my operations in all three cities. Therefore, we make them pay by hitting them again. We get some vengeance.'

Javier cleared his throat. 'That could work.'

'Only this time we don't fuck around. This time we hit them hard and where it hurts. And we don't do it three times, we hit them ten times. We step up the game.'

Javier's mouth worked, but no words came out. He appeared nonplussed.

'We let them know it's in retaliation for the foiled chemical attacks. We let them *know* who's behind it and that it's all their fault. That will teach them to hinder me.'

'It's a bold plan. Do you think we can pull it off?'

'I want my vengeance. I am the Dark Tsar, a terrorist super-king. I am a ghost. Nobody ruins my plans. Do you hear? My assets are limitless.'

'Did you have something in mind?'

'Oh, yes. And it wouldn't even be that hard to set up. But I want the authorities to know all about it. I want them to feel it coming, to run scared, to strike fear into the entire population. I want that fear to be global.'

'I don't quite follow.'

'Oh, you will, Javier. You will.' The tsar fixed himself another drink, now feeling the glow. It was working for him. He ran ideas through his head, formulated plans. The feeling of ignominious defeat was rapidly changing, and he liked it.

'This starts with us,' he said rapidly. 'We send our people to the ten cities. Send them fast. We give them resources, let them procure the ordinance. This all has to be done within a few weeks. It must look like a quick retaliation, but we can't do it any faster than that. When the authorities find out what they've done, and what they've wrought, they will fall apart. Shit themselves. They will know they've fucked up and there's nothing they can do but reap the whirlwind. And Javier... I *am* that whirlwind.'

'You want to get started right away, don't you? How about a couple of hookers to get us in the mood?'

The tsar waved him away. 'Go get laid if you want to. I have a lot of planning to do.'

But Javier wouldn't leave his friend's and boss's side. He would remain there, because he knew that, really, he was needed.

The Dark Tsar threw himself behind his desk and took out a thick notebook and a pen. 'Now,' he said. 'This is gonna take some planning.'

CHAPTER SIXTEEN

Time passed, a few days. Drake returned to Washington, DC, with his team and went back to their homes. The biggest thing on their plate was the upcoming funeral of Connor Bryant.

A few days before, they all met up. Their bruises were healing, the events that followed Bryant's death now fully at the backs of their minds. Drake and Alicia walked to a nearby coffee shop and took a few tables outside, waiting for their friends to join them. It felt good to be back in DC, relaxing after the stresses of combat, but already they were wondering what was coming next.

When they were all together, Hayden spoke up. 'I've been asking around Glacier, trying to find out what the hell happens next. It's chaos. With Bryant gone, there's a big hole in the company. Now apparently, two of the surviving shareholders will take control of the company and start running the day-to-day business. I don't know these shareholders. I've never even met them. There's no personal connection whatsoever. Already, I'm not feeling it.'

Drake sat back. Lately, Hayden had also been angling for them to go solo. They'd all talked about it, spit balling, not really serious, but Hayden seemed to embrace it more every day.

'It won't be the same without Bryant at the helm,' Dahl said, also interested in the solo project.

'Because he threw us the best jobs?' Alicia asked.

'Well, I did feel kind of special,' Dahl smiled. 'But, in truth, he knew what we thrived on. The type of jobs we would excel at. I'm not sure I want to be told what to do by a couple of shareholders.'

Drake felt the same way, but maybe that was all because of change. Nobody liked change. As a team, they were set in their ways.

'It could change everything,' Kenzie said.

'A change could be as good as a rest,' Shaw said. 'Embrace it.'

'I'm too long in the tooth for that crap,' Drake said jokingly.

'Either way,' Hayden said. 'If we go solo, or if we stay with Glacier, there will be change.'

'I want to go solo,' Cam said. 'Think of the new jobs we could get.'

The discussion turned around Glacier and solo. Drake noticed Mai was particularly quiet. Bryant's funeral was tomorrow. He knew there was nothing he could do for her. She was still grieving and would be for quite some time. The only upside was that they had found Soroyan and, through him, foiled three terrible attacks. And all that through the death of Connor Bryant. It was a harsh, strange world sometimes.

'We have the contacts,' Kinimaka was saying. 'To get recommended for jobs. Once we've done a few, we'll get the reputation. We'll be able to write our own ticket.'

'We've already got the reputation,' Dahl said. 'In

the right circles. You know it. Everyone knows what the Spear team did, what the Ghost Squadron has done. We just have to remind them.'

'You're really up for the solo gig?' Drake asked him.

The Swede nodded. 'Going forward, it's the best bet. Long term – it's our pension.'

Drake hadn't thought about it that way. Truth be told, he hadn't even considered how they'd manage as they grew older. He sipped his coffee, considering.

'There is the issue of money,' Hayden said. 'I'm guessing we all have savings?'

They all nodded. In their line of work, there wasn't a lot of spare time to spend money on things. Drake himself had a fair few quid saved up.

'We could get by for a few months,' he said. 'Tide us over until the real money rolls in.'

'We'd need an office, insurance, weapons, some kind of contract,' Mai now pointed out. 'There's a lot of work to do before we put boots on the ground.'

'Might even need a few employees,' Alicia said with a grin. 'A few hunky lads should do the trick.'

Drake stared across at her. 'I'm right here.'

'Don't worry. I'll still have time for you as well.'

The morning passed quickly, eventfully, as the Ghost Squadron considered their future now that Glacier's own future was uncertain. The sun shone down on them, dappling them in shadow, and they were content, knowing they had no missions to do, no bad guys to catch. There was no talk of the Dark Tsar, of what might have happened. They were happy knowing someone else was dealing with that problem.

***

Drake stood at the graveside, eyes downcast. It was a dull, blustery day, brown leaves scuttling along the narrow pathways and grassy areas. Concrete gravestones stood all around and there was a second funeral happening not too far away. Drake listened as the vicar spoke, as the wind blew, and as the distant hum of road traffic counterpointed the speech.

I've been to too many of these, he thought.

Mai stood to his right, tears in her eyes. Drake had an arm around her. To his left stood Alicia, equally sombre. The rest of the team were all around, supporting with their presence. The vicar spoke for ten minutes and then the guests paid their respects and then started walking away. Drake wasn't surprised to see many of Bryant's work colleagues present. He had been a good boss.

They all met afterwards in some establishment that Drake neither knew nor cared to know. He stayed close to Mai, offering help where he could, but the Japanese woman was as strong as they came, and was able to get through it all. It was only later, when they were all together at Hayden's home, that she showed her true feelings.

'I'm gonna miss him so much,' she said, tears in her eyes. 'I don't know what to do with myself.'

Drake sat on the arm of the chair beside her. 'He was a good man. One of the best. I'm gonna miss him.'

Dahl came over. 'Whatever you need, Mai. Whatever you need.'

The evening passed in sombre cheer. They tried to

celebrate Bryant's life, to stay upbeat about all he'd achieved, but the attempt fell flat. They just couldn't believe they'd lost another member of their team. Midnight came and went and still the team was sitting around, chatting quietly. By the time the sun dawned, nobody had moved.

The next few days passed miserably, and then an entire week had gone by since they foiled the attacks. The team fell into a kind of supportive habit, meeting for breakfast, drinking their coffee and eating their pastries together, ready to lend a hand to Mai if she needed it. They met in the afternoons and went out, sometimes even met up for an evening meal. Normally, when they were off-mission, the team stayed away from each other, to get a little space. But not this time, not through these dark days.

More days came and went. It didn't get any easier, but life went on and they were forced to deal with it. Hayden threw herself even deeper into the solo project along with Kinimaka, the two of them immersing themselves in all the pros and cons. The office contacted them, promising no change to their work environment, but offering no mission. Drake wasn't sure if he'd accept a mission at this time, in any case.

The hours passed slowly. The days were dark, full of drizzle, matching their mood. They visited Bryant's grave as a team, as a supportive group.

Almost two weeks had passed when Hayden approached them. They were seated inside their usual breakfast café, a big airy place with outsize round tables. There was rain on the windows and coating the slick streets. The clouds were low, and the morning was dank and dark. The day felt like an outer expression of their hearts.

'This downtime,' she said. 'Has been put to good use. I think it's time we came to a decision.'

Drake picked up his croissant and took a bite. 'I know you've been hard at work researching the new solo project.'

'All aspects. We don't need government approval specifically. We do need special licenses. I have all the information we need and I've researched it thoroughly.'

'We have,' Mano Kinimaka put in.

'Yes, we have. Now, do you want to hear me out?' She looked mostly at Mai, as if to check talking about normal, everyday life was all right. Mai gave her a brief smile and a nod.

Hayden started talking. They got their drinks refilled. Kinimaka and Dahl both ordered more pastries. Hayden ran everything by them and then finished with the words, 'Glacier hasn't exactly been calling us every day with a new op.'

Drake had been thinking the same thing. They were entirely out of the loop now, unable to call Bryant to see what was going on. Their umbilical cord into Glacier's inner workings had been severed. Even Bryant's second-in-command had been left in the dark by the new operators.

'We're still getting paid,' Alicia pointed out practically. 'They're bound to assign us something sooner or later.'

'You lose the edge,' Dahl said. 'You know that.'

Alicia nodded gloomily. Hayden was looking around the group expectantly. 'What are your thoughts?'

'I think we should go for it,' Dahl said. 'I'm up for the challenge.'

One by one, the team agreed to her proposition. Cam and Shaw, always looking for a test, were up for it straight away. Kenzie voiced a few concerns, but was pretty much convinced. Drake agreed with Dahl because if they stayed on the sidelines too long, they would lose their edge in battle. Alicia seemed happy with the idea.

Which left Mai.

The Japanese woman sighed. 'I feel like parting with Glacier is like parting with the last vestiges of Bryant. I know it's ridiculous.'

'Not ridiculous at all,' Drake said. 'I get it.'

Mai sighed at him and then looked at Hayden. Finally, she smiled. 'Let's do it,' she said. 'Let's start our own private company and make Bryant proud.'

Hayden sat back, a cheerful expression on her face. The team all looked at each other, energised. Something new was on the way.

CHAPTER SEVENTEEN

Two weeks had passed. Drake and the others were at Hayden's house, discussing how the new venture might work. The team were seeing a long gestation period in which they might not be able to work as they pulled things together... thus making everything harder. And the admin side of the business... that didn't suit any of them.

The day before, Patrick Sutherland, the assistant director of the FBI, had called them. He spoke via Hayden's speakerphone.

'Just a quick update for you,' he said. 'You helped to stop the attacks, so I think you deserve to stay in the loop. We've put – and are putting – significant resources into learning about this so called Dark Tsar and, so far, have come up with very little. All we know is that he appears to exist. He doesn't do business with any of the usual subjects – the people we might know. He doesn't run in the circles we know. Doesn't appear to have a wider network. If he is operating somewhere in the world, he keeps everything in-house, close to his chest and uses middle-men who aren't aware who's pulling the strings. A very clever operation.'

'I wonder how he reacted when his latest plan was thwarted,' Dahl said.

'I wonder why the hell he planned it in the first place,' Drake said. 'Doesn't seem right for a so-called ghost.'

'Probably wanted to change things up a bit,' Kinimaka said. 'Probably bored. You know what these crazy megalomaniac types are like.'

With that, Sutherland signed off and left them to it. They tried to put all dire thoughts of the Dark Tsar out of their minds.

Now, they worked on their new project. They'd been seeing an awful lot of each other this last week, getting on each other's nerves, and the relationships were a little strained. Drake wondered how that would pan out in the future. This was an entirely new work environment for them.

They weren't worried about getting jobs. They had contacts, lots of them, not the least of which was Michael Crouch, Drake's old boss. Crouch had one of the best contact networks in the world and would love to be of help. Drake and Alicia had already spoken extensively to him.

'How do we move this forward?' Hayden was saying. 'You know, I think we might even have to split up for some jobs.'

Drake didn't like the sound of that, but knew it had been coming. 'If a job requires three people,' he said. 'How are we gonna decide who goes?'

'Toss for it,' Dahl said.

'I'd like to see that,' Alicia said with a grin.

'Whoever suits it,' Hayden said with a shrug. 'If it requires a hero, we'll send Dahl. If it requires-'

'If it requires a hooker, we'll send Alicia,' Kenzie grinned.

'And if it requires an emotionless bitch.' Alicia nodded at the other woman.

Hayden tried to keep the conversation pertinent. 'Like I said, we all decide on who goes to what. And I'm sure there'll be a job that will require all of us.'

'The sooner we get started, the better,' Drake said. Still, they had not heard from Glacier. It was as if they'd been cast out into the wilderness. He sat back on Hayden's sofa, worrying about the team's lack of action, their overall fitness, their mental health.

And then the phone rang.

Hayden glanced at it, startled, then punched a button. 'Hello?'

'This is Patrick Sutherland. Is the whole team with you?'

'They're all here, sir.'

'Good. Listen up. A terrorist calling himself the Dark Tsar has bombed two hospitals in Europe. He says it's in retaliation for preventing his earlier chemical attacks.'

Drake felt a weakness pass through him. The weakness of fear. 'Hospitals?' he repeated.

'Yes. It's his form of revenge, apparently. But it's not just that. His message has gone out publicly. All the world knows. The pressure is building.'

'Why the hell would he come out of hiding this way?' Hayden asked.

'There's more, and it's bad. Really bad. The Dark Tsar has publicly declared that his vengeance will consist of bombing *ten* hospitals, two every week, unless we can stop him. He's issued a challenge, really.'

Drake felt like he was being bombarded. The hits

kept coming, and there was nowhere to hide. The team were all staring at the phone in shock.

'Ten?' Mai said. 'Hospitals?'

'It's a challenge to the safety of the world,' Sutherland said.

'There's no ransom? No demand?' Dahl asked.

'That's one of the scariest parts,' Sutherland said. 'No demands at all. He's just defying us. Daring us to catch him.'

Drake wondered then why Sutherland was calling them personally. He had the entire FBI at his disposal. 'Is there something in particular we can help you with?' He asked.

'I'm glad you asked. You're my failsafe. I'm assembling a lot of teams as well as the usual forces, and I want you to be one of them. One of my redundancies. We're putting everything into this.'

'What do you want us to do?'

'First, there's a briefing and I want you to be there. After that, you'll get your assignments.'

Drake was already on his feet. He looked around, saw nods and affirmations on everyone's faces. He said, 'Just tell us where to go.'

CHAPTER EIGHTEEN

Sutherland informed them a huge and terrible scramble was ensuing. All the world's security forces were mobilising to stop the Dark Tsar. In DC, it was no different. Drake and the others were asked to attend a briefing immediately.

They didn't hesitate. Just picked up their jackets and left the café. They ordered Ubers and took a tense journey into the heart of the city where they were ushered into the blocky, grey concrete FBI building and shown to a large room. Here they took their seats, waiting to be addressed. The room was packed with men and women, some standing, some milling around, others leaning against the walls. Some were armed, and others carried thick folders and many talked in clusters, all grave. It was a sombre, busy, noisy room. Drake and the team just sat there, knowing nobody and getting curious glances. Twenty minutes passed. More people were arriving all the time. Soon, for the newcomers, it was standing room only, and then the doors were locked. Drake and the others sat expectantly.

Finally, Patrick Sutherland made his way to the raised platform at the front of the room. He stood behind a lectern and spoke into the microphone.

'Hello everyone,' he said. 'We all know why we're

here. Now, I'm going to tell you everything we know about this madman, this Dark Tsar, who has issued the threat. First, let me tell you that meetings like this are taking place all across the world, in London, in Paris, in Berlin. Everywhere.'

Sutherland cleared his throat.

'The Dark Tsar is a European male. He's supposedly tall, short, bearded, non-bearded and has a bald head with lots of hair. His eyes are between blue, black and brown. He's fit, unhealthy, dying. Not only that, but he's a womaniser, a loner and a cheat. *That's* precisely what we know about him.'

There was a stunned silence around the room, people looking at each other. Nobody spoke.

'So you see,' Sutherland went on. 'The Dark Tsar is a mystery. Nobody knows who he is, where he lives, who he deals with. Until recently, he was considered a myth even inside our own intelligence agencies. I say all this to impress upon you how dangerous and capable this man is.'

Drake wondered how they were going to handle it. Already, he thought, there had to be thousands of enquiries reaching out around the world – everyone searching for this Dark Tsar.

'So far, he's bombed the two hospitals in Europe,' Sutherland went on. 'He's promised eight more, two per week simultaneously, unless we stop him. That's it. No demands, no ransom. This guy actually wants us to take him down. Or...' he shrugged. 'He's baiting us. He believes we won't be able to catch him. Well, we have teams in every major city gearing up to do just that. And now we have you. Get ready for your assignments.'

One by one, people circulated around the room. Certain individuals were given folders and started leafing through them. Drake sat expectantly, wondering what they'd be given. Soon, though, all the folders had been handed out and the Ghost Squadron sat empty-handed. Sutherland spoke for another twenty minutes and then dismissed them, warning them all that they had to report everything to their line managers, no matter how trivial, how unimportant it seemed. The world's security forces would live or die on their next actions. They couldn't let this man beat them. Hold them over a barrel. They couldn't let him win, or another dozen like him would crawl out of the woodwork. Not to mention the civilian losses.

Drake and the others sat patiently whilst people started filing out of the room. Finally, Sutherland came up to them.

'Glad you came,' he said, turning a seat around so that he could sit in front of them. 'It's like trying to start the world's biggest juggernaut and getting it moving on ice,' he sighed. 'We haven't mobilised anything this big in years.'

'What do you want from us?' Hayden asked.

'Unfortunately, nothing. I can't use you yet. You're civilian contractors, as it were. I *want* to use you, for sure. But I can't just yet.'

He was looking directly at them, his eyebrows raised. Was he trying to tell them something? Finally, he said. 'Wait, just wait. Let the juggernaut do its work. Then... we'll see.'

Drake bit his lower lip. 'Wait?'

Sutherland nodded. 'That's the best I can do for

now. I wanted you to be part of this meeting so you know where we're at and what we're doing. But I can't involve you yet. We have to let the proper security forces do their thing.'

Drake wasn't sure he liked that. Did that mean they were *im*proper? Well, maybe that was closer to the truth than he'd initially believed. Were they a ragtag team? Did they possess the professionalism to successfully run their own company? This was a thought that hadn't occurred to him until now. He looked Sutherland in the eye.

'You're benching us because we're not part of the system anymore?'

'You got it. But I want you on standby. I fear I may need your help, and soon.'

With that, Sutherland rose and walked out of the room. Drake stared at his friends, feeling let down and lost. He didn't quite know what to say.

'After that, after everything he's told us, he's now telling us to go home,' Kinimaka said. 'That sucks.'

'Big time,' Kenzie said. 'Now I'm on a downer.'

They were the last people in the room. Drake led them towards the door. Once outside, they threaded a few hallways and then left the building. It was as cold outside as he felt on the inside. He shivered.

'Sutherland wants us to wait,' he said. 'We wait. He's running the show.'

'Usually, we're in the thick of it all,' Dahl said. 'Running the show, knocking doors down. They send us in first. Now... it's all changed.'

'We don't work for them anymore, and Glacier's not part of this,' Drake said. 'As much as I hate to say it... we're sidelined.'

CHAPTER NINETEEN

They were updated regularly to keep them in the loop. It was torture. Drake had never felt anything like it. The others voiced similar emotions, and none of them slept easy. A day passed and then another. Updates told them the world's security forces were no closer to finding the Dark Tsar. People were beyond edgy; they were beside themselves. How could everyone draw a blank?

But leads came up, and they were followed. Drake and the team were told about a raid in Geneva, where a special forces team assaulted a large mansion two miles from the lake. It all went off without a hitch, but the man they found knew nothing. It seemed one of his rivals had ratted him out for the hell of it. The man they caught revealed nothing of the Dark Tsar, even under harsh interrogation.

Then there was the raid in Manchester, UK. A gang was thought to have ties to one of the Tsar's operations. A huge team secured the gang. It was successful, but the gang was clueless. They worked for many people, some of the leaders a dozen times removed from the deals that were actually going down. The gang itself didn't know and didn't care who they, ultimately, worked for. The actual gang leader was as helpful as he could be under pressure, but, in the end, knew nothing.

A third raid took place in Copenhagen. An arms dealer was investigated and looked to be getting the bulk of his goods from a shady, suspicious character in Prague. This tied in with another contact, who told them the Dark Tsar had ties to Prague. The raid was again successful as a whole. The attack caused many casualties on both sides and, ultimately, proved fruitless, since the arms dealer knew nothing.

'Are they pushing them enough?' Dahl asked, as they heard about the latest failure.

'You mean torturing them if needs be?' Sutherland's aide said. 'Rest assured, the matter is serious enough to take all actions.'

'I wish I was involved,' Dahl said. 'I'd get the information, believe me.'

Overnight, more raids took place. Security forces in Britain, France and Belgium struck relentlessly on their quest to hunt down the Dark Tsar. In all three locations, local, prominent criminals were targeted, captured, interrogated. And in all three locations, the information was shown to be inaccurate.

All leads led nowhere.

On the second morning, the team met in their favourite café. There was a feeling of powerlessness in the air.

'I'm not liking this,' Drake said. 'The days are passing. They're getting nowhere. I mean, there's plenty getting done, but we're no further forward.'

'It all seems to be red herrings,' Alicia said.

Just before they'd arrived, they'd received another update from one of Sutherland's aides. During the early morning, a team in DC itself had acted. They'd received credible information that a criminal overlord had strong ties to a devious figure again in Prague. The attack had proven successful, though again casualties were suffered, but the overlord knew nothing. Drake was starting to wonder if they were concentrating too heavily on Prague.

'It *is* all red herrings,' he said. 'And it wouldn't surprise me if the Dark Tsar had planted most of them to help cultivate his mystery. Obviously, he's been at this for years. He knows exactly what he's doing.'

'And still we're not involved,' Dahl grumbled.

Hayden's phone buzzed. She answered it, listened for a while, and then thanked the caller. She looked around, eyes sad. 'It gets worse,' she said. 'And it seems to be escalating. A team in Paris got information that the Tsar had some dealings with a local prostitution gang. It seemed legit. They tracked the headquarters of this gang down, got ready, and then hit it,' she sighed. 'The damn place was booby trapped. It went up like a torch. The lead, it seems, was planted.'

'By the Dark Tsar?' Cam asked.

'It seems so. He's now actively leading the security forces into traps.'

'A fresh development,' Drake said. 'We can't just sit around and watch this happen.'

'That's exactly what we've been told to do,' Hayden said. 'By the assistant director of the FBI. You want to go against his orders?'

'It crossed my mind,' Dahl said quickly.

'We can't,' Hayden said. 'It's not like we're fully out of the loop. We're getting constant updates. So... that proves we're in his plans.'

'I just think we're the one team that can do something about this,' Drake said. 'Look at our track record.'

'The best team frozen out,' Alicia said. 'It seems odd.'

'If we were still team SPEAR, we'd be in the thick of it,' Kinimaka said. *'Because* we worked for a government agency. We don't do that anymore.'

Drake felt impotent, at a loss. Could they go against Sutherland's orders? What the hell could they do, anyway? He looked at Hayden. 'Are you on the fence with this?'

'There's no fence,' she said. 'It's black and white. Sutherland didn't have to get us involved with this. He chose to. If he wants us, he'll call.'

'I think we should move forward on our own,' Dahl said.

Drake took a moment to think, sipping his black coffee. It wasn't often that there was contention in the ranks.

'I guess we take a vote,' he said.

He sat back as the team voted. In the end, Dahl, Kenzie, and Alicia were the only ones who voted for action. Everyone else wanted to wait for Sutherland's word. The three didn't like it, but they accepted without further questions.

The rest of the day passed, and they stuck together. Twice more Hayden's phone rang and there were reports of more failed raids.

Another in Prague, where two security teams attacked a mansion that housed several drug dealers. The Dark Tsar was supposed to be buying produce from there. Nothing came of the raid, and more men died during the attack. The Dark Tsar was laughing at them.

The second call told them of another booby trapped building. Luckily, on this occasion, the team suffered no casualties. But they also came away empty-handed, with no further information.

The day passed. Nobody slept that night. Drake and Alicia spent hours talking or staring at the ceiling, worrying about the teams out in the world, trying their best to locate the Dark Tsar. They felt ineffective, feeble. There was nothing they could do. All Drake wanted was to get that phone call from Sutherland. The call that would call them to action.

The days were passing too quickly as the world itself waited with bated breath. Because the tsar had relayed his message publicly, all the world's press were involved and the reports of failure were hitting the headlines every day, every hour. Information was leaked to the press even at the best of times and, now, it was leaked with abandon.

And the world's press jumped eagerly all over it.

Drake and the others couldn't turn on a TV or thumb through their phone without seeing the terrible, eye-catching reports. The press were milking it for all it was worth, revelling in it, showering forth their clickbait.

As an early morning sun rose to paint its first rays onto the curtains of their bedroom, Drake turned to Alicia.

'I don't know what the hell to do,' he said.

CHAPTER TWENTY

'Are we definitely doing this?' Alicia asked.

Drake stared at her. 'You wanted this yesterday, and the day before.'

'I want us all to agree. No regrets.'

Drake took in a deep breath and nodded. 'I think it's the only way to go.'

Following more reports of failure and deadly traps, they had met up that morning and decided to start conducting an investigation of their own. It was what the Ghost Squadron had to do. They weren't passive or docile. Never had been. Part of their success revolved around being forceful, active, powerful. They weren't the sort of team who could stand around waiting for someone to tell them what to do.

And Dahl, Alicia, and some others believed Sutherland was well aware of that.

'All right,' Hayden said. 'What's the plan?'

Hayden had been the least convinced of all of them, but she had relented eventually. In her heart, she believed they had to act.

'The only plan is to find this Dark Tsar as soon as possible,' Drake said. 'And not impede the world's security forces. We have to do this our way.'

'And what way is that?' Shaw asked.

'We're starting with nothing, starting blind,' Drake said. 'But we have options. There are good people we know who work at Glacier, talented investigators. There's Steve Redding, Bryant's second in charge. And then there's Michael Crouch.'

'You sure we shouldn't wait for Sutherland?' Hayden asked.

Drake spread his arms. 'We've waited long enough.'

The work began. They called Redding first and asked him to start making enquiries using the firm's resources. They were looking for any information relating to the Dark Tsar, but especially from company mercenaries who may have worked for him. It was amazing what you could find out from a disgruntled mercenary. And, let's face it, Drake thought, mercenaries are always disgruntled, never believing they earned enough pay.

Redding was amenable and said he'd get started right away. Drake asked him to keep the whole thing under his hat until it was time to call him back.

Next, there were two special investigators who worked for Glacier. Drake and Hayden called them up, asked for their help in locating the Dark Tsar. There were misgivings at first, and a touch of fear. These guys had been present when the building was attacked and didn't want to shed any light on themselves. In the end, though, they agreed and said they'd put substantial resources behind their search.

Through all this, the team weren't expecting to find anything that the world's security services hadn't, but they believed they had a unique take on the search. They could ask in places where others couldn't and be privy to more personal information.

Finally, they called Michael Crouch, the man who'd helped them out countless times before and worked with them on several occasions. Drake made the call in Hayden's house and then laid the phone on the table, switching to speakerphone.

'Ay up, Michael,' he said. 'What's happening?'

Once the small talk was done, they got down to business.

'No doubt you'll have heard about this new wanker,' Drake said. 'This Dark Tsar who's holding the world to ransom?'

Crouch affirmed he had.

'We're invested in finding him, mate. We're directing all our resources at it. The guy seems to be a ghost. And we're getting close to the next deadline.'

'Did you know I'd retired?'

Drake was taken aback. 'I didn't know that, mate. And Alicia certainly never told me.'

'Well, to be fair, Alicia wouldn't know. I retired after our last escapade in Hawaii.'

'It was probably working with Alicia that did it,' Kenzie said.

Alicia gave her the finger.

Drake didn't quite know what to say. 'So you're out of the game? For good?'

Crouch coughed. 'I'm supposed to be,' he sighed. 'But I find it harder to relax in retirement than I did when I was working. There's always something needs doing.'

Drake wasn't sure if he should apologise or carry on. He decided on the latter. 'You have the best contacts in the world, Michael.'

There was another sigh. 'How important is this to you?'

'We're privy to all the information but not allowed to act,' Hayden said. 'You know how much we want to stop this guy. It's the kind of thing we do.'

'We're essentially frozen out,' Alicia said. 'Can't act until Sutherland says we can. But maybe he expects us to do something on the quiet. I know I would. And, honestly, I don't think he can legally involve us.'

'Patrick Sutherland of the FBI?'

'Yeah, that's him.'

'He's a connection of mine. I could reach out. Ask him to get you involved?'

Hayden took that one. 'I think we've kinda decided we want to do this our way.'

'Our way's the best,' Alicia said with a grin.

'Oh, I know all about that,' Crouch said with irony. 'I've been a part of it several times.'

Drake thought the conversation was heading in the right direction. 'So, you'll help us?'

Crouch didn't hesitate. 'Of course. I've stayed out of this entire business until now. But I'll happily get stuck in for you.'

'Anything you can get,' Kinimaka said. 'Anything we can use.'

'I get the idea.'

Crouch ended the call, and they sat there in Hayden's front room, staring at each other. Now they had people working for them, trying to dig up information.

'I feel better about it,' Drake said. 'At least we're not just sitting here twiddling out thumbs.'

It didn't make the waiting any easier. They sat back, unsure what to do. Alicia wanted to chase their contacts almost immediately, but Drake knew they'd call when they had something. He overruled the Englishwoman, much to her chagrin.

First one hour passed and then another. The team talked and stared out the window and made sure they knew where their gear was stowed in case they could soon make use of it. The chances of that were remote, since the Dark Tsar was almost certainly based somewhere in Europe or the far east and that would require a plane journey. They'd have to secure more gear when they arrived, and probably in a subtle way. It had been so much easier when they worked for the government and could use the various arms stashes.

They ate dinner. Darkness fell. They were ready to go. Still nothing from their contacts. Drake felt the suspense building. There was a pent-up energy inside him, something that needed to be released. It was the same for all of them. When eight p.m. passed, Drake went and fixed himself a drink. He stared around at the others.

'Sutherland waited too long,' he said ominously. 'Tomorrow's the first deadline day.'

They all knew it. Nobody answered him. They split up, left Hayden's house, and returned to their own. It was hard work getting to sleep that night.

Morning dawned and there was still no word from their contacts. Instead, they called Sutherland and left a message. Today was a bad day, and they'd not received any updates in twenty-four hours.

Again, the time crawled by. Minutes grew into

long hours. The team decided not to meet but kept in touch through text, assuring each other they'd call if they heard something. It was around midday when Crouch called Drake.

'It's me,' he said without introduction. 'I'm balls deep in this now. Took me most of the night to call everyone I know. So far, I have nothing for you, but just wanted to let you know. These things can take time.'

'The one thing we don't have,' Drake said. 'Today's a deadline day.'

'I know. I'll come back to you as soon as I can.'

Drake and Alicia looked at each other with dejected looks in their eyes. There was fear too, fear of what was to come. Quickly, they let the others know through a group message. Once again, the hours passed agonisingly slowly.

Drake and Alicia didn't watch TV much, but they had it on today, tuned to a news channel. When a breaking news banner flashed up, they turned all their attention to the screen. Drake turned it up.

'We're getting reports of a tremendous explosion in Germany. And…' the newsreader put her finger to her ear. '… and another one in France. Two hospitals are involved. This does seem to be the work of the notorious Dark Tsar, making good on his promise. We await further developments and will bring them to you as they occur.'

Drake had never felt so impotent. If only they'd been involved from the start, they might have prevented this. They'd have made a difference at the very least. They were the best at what they did.

Why not let us help?

Alicia turned away from the screen. The pressure on the authorities would now be unbearable. The Dark Tsar wasn't just beating them as he murdered the innocent, he was laughing at them again and again. Telling them they were weak, ineffectual, spineless. And there was nothing they could do about it.

Drake continued to watch the TV. About an hour after the first report, the screen flashed to a paused YouTube upload with the newsreader talking over the frozen screen.

'This video was uploaded to the Dark Web and also passed along to several news channels. We're about to play it for you now but warn you it contains upsetting information.'

The picture unfroze. Drake saw a figure shrouded in darkness. A silhouette. The unknown man started speaking.

'Seven days have passed. You have shown how weak you are; that you cannot find me. So now I have extracted another day of vengeance. I have targeted two more hospitals, as you will be aware. This is an action you yourselves wrought. I am not to blame. *You* thought you had beat me, that you had stopped the Dark Tsar. *You* thought you had won. I'm showing you today that you lost, and that you lost badly. There are six more hospitals to go. I challenge you to stop me.'

The video ended, the screen cutting momentarily to black. Drake shook his head, realising his hands were bunched into fists. His knuckles were white. Alicia stood next to him, a dark expression on her face.

'We must find that bastard,' she said. 'And show him that the Ghost Squadron can destroy his world.'

Drake agreed. In the next few minutes, he found himself on a group telephone call, but even that didn't help. There was nothing they could do. Not yet. They had to hope that their contacts came through with something.

And they had to hope it happened soon.

CHAPTER TWENTY ONE

Patrick Sutherland's aide rang them a couple of hours later. Again, there was no news. The Dark Tsar was a terrible enigma, a mystery blight on the world. Hayden felt it appropriate to tell the aide they were working on his capture too and hoped he'd pass the news on to Sutherland. Maybe Sutherland had been hoping for that all along.

It was late in the afternoon when Crouch finally called them. He'd given them a warning, asked that they all be together and that he be put on speakerphone.

'Everyone,' he began. 'You're not going to like what I have to tell you.'

They were again gathered at Hayden's house, sitting around the front room. Drake was leaning by the window and spoke up first.

'I don't think we expected to, mate.'

'It's worse than you can imagine,' Crouch went on. 'As you know, my contacts are far-reaching, universal. I can learn anything about anyone in the shortest period. I have men and women everywhere, willing to help me. But this Dark Tsar... he is the hardest person I have ever had to find. And by all accounts, he is the worst.'

'We know that already,' Dahl said quietly.

'My contacts have started coming back to me. It is difficult for them. Most of them are on site, so to speak, working. And most of them are scared. Some have even been approached by the authorities already and turned them down.'

'They're in terrible danger,' Mai said. 'We all are.'

'You're about to be,' Crouch said. 'If you decide to pursue this. Are you sure you want to go ahead?'

Drake knew nobody on the team would back down and, to be fair, so did Crouch. But he had to ask the question. 'We're all in,' he said.

'All right, then. This is the extent of my enquiries. I've found out that you won't get anywhere near the Dark Tsar. He's too well guarded.'

'We can get close to anyone,' Alicia said. They had done it before.

'Not this guy. Not in a one-off strike, if that's what you were thinking. Even if you could find out where he's located – which you can't – he's always surrounded by many guards. A strike wouldn't work.'

'Is there another way?' Drake asked. He had to assume Crouch was building up to something.

'There may be,' Crouch said. 'But it will be the most dangerous thing you've ever done.'

Drake blinked. 'We've been in some pretty precarious situations, mate.'

'Oh, I know. But this is next level. And it will take time. That's the other problem.'

'Longer than a week?' Drake was conscious of the next deadline.

'Maybe. That all depends on unknown factors.'

'What's your suggestion?' Hayden asked.

'Your only option is to penetrate the Tsar's

organisation from the outside in. It's all you can do and, yes, there are several ways. You can't do it as a team. There's too many of you. So you'll have to do it in twos and threes. Separately. And it's going to be nigh on impossible.'

'From the outside?' Drake repeated. 'You mean to ingratiate ourselves with his various operations? Worm our way in? Won't that take months?'

'Not the way I've planned it. I've found places to insert you that have direct links to the tsar, or the tsar's location. If you're good enough, you can get invited to go join him.'

'Can't you just give us that?' Alicia asked.

'It's a closely guarded secret, as you can imagine. You only find out when you arrive. And then, I'm told, you don't really know where you are. You're not allowed outside.'

'If we're good enough, hey?' Alicia said. 'What do you mean by that?'

'You have to prove that the Tsar can't do without you. That you're an essential cog in his organisation. And you have to do that in a few days.'

The team stared at each other, eyes narrowing. Dahl whistled. 'What could be easier?' he said with sarcasm.

'As I said, it's going to be hard. But, if anyone can do it, you can. You will need to get to the absolute heart of the Tsar's operation in order to get close to him.'

'And how do you think we can do that?' Shaw asked.

'Can't you guess?'

'Oh, I can,' Alicia said.

'And you're probably right. The whole team is going to have to go undercover.'

Drake had guessed that already. 'Do you have several ingress points for us?'

Crouch coughed. 'Yeah, I've made the arrangements. You'll have to decide who goes where and with whom.'

'Do you have any more info on this guy?' Drake asked. 'Anything that can help us?'

'I'll get to that. First, I have to know if you're all up for the undercover assignments. I have to firm up arrangements.'

Drake looked swiftly around the room but didn't really need to check. 'We're all up for it,' he said.

'Good, then I'll call you back shortly. Once I put this in place, guys, you're going to have to move fast and it will be a rollercoaster ride all the way to the finish.'

Drake thanked him and hung up. He stared at his friends. So much waiting, so much anxiety, and soon they'd be racing towards a very uncertain end.

'Once we're undercover,' he said. 'Every second will be dangerous. Take care of yourselves and don't do anything stupid.'

That brought a few smiles. Drake could sense some anxiety, too. They weren't exactly experienced in undercover work, especially Cam and Shaw. The others, he knew, would all have some knowledge of it.

'Talk about a tough assignment,' Shaw said. 'I've never done anything like it.'

Cam put his hand on hers. 'You'll crush it. We'll do it together.'

'We might all decide who our partners are gonna be,' Drake said. 'Depending on what the assignments are, I suppose.'

The phone rang.

CHAPTER TWENTY TWO

This time, it wasn't Crouch on the line.

It was their contacts in Bryant's office, the two investigators. They appeared to have a different take on things, and had worked the problem differently.

The first man, Anderson, spoke up. 'We've come at the issue from another angle. We thought we'd question our resident staff about the Dark Tsar himself. See what we can find out about him.'

Drake knew that by resident staff, they meant mercenaries. 'Great idea,' he said. 'I assume you've had some luck?'

'Quite a bit actually,' the other man, Creswell, said. 'Of all the men and women we asked, over half a dozen have worked indirectly for the Tsar. And some of these have worked with people who work *directly* with him. And you know how mercs gossip to anyone but the authorities.'

Drake looked at Dahl. 'Yeah, I know so well.'

The Swede gave him the double finger. 'What do you have?'

'All right, then. Well, it seems the Tsar is an alpha male who loves beautiful women. Could be a weakness. He surrounds himself with them and, unless he's working, always has one draped across him. Apparently. And even when he's working, they're not far away.'

'So he loves his women,' Drake said. 'That's interesting. Anything else?'

'Oh, yeah. Besides being a bit of a playboy, he loves his forties music. It's played all the time, apparently. Non stop. Pisses all the mercs off.'

Drake couldn't see how that might help, but appreciated the effort nonetheless. 'Anything else?' he asked.

'Yeah,' Anderson said. 'The dude loves his fine dining. Has a few top chefs working for him and gets real upset if the fodder isn't up to the right standard. He's a stickler, apparently. No waffles and chicken nuggets for this guy.'

'So he loves women, forties music and fine dining,' Kinimaka said. 'What else?'

'You can probably already guess this, but he's a perfectionist. Nothing but the best will do. And he expects that from all his employees, too. And what he says goes. You follow his orders to the letter... or else.'

'There are rumours,' Creswell went on. 'Rumours about all the terrible deeds he's been involved in. The guy has been a player since he was young. Worked his way up through the ranks and then became the man in charge. Ever since he seized power, he's wielded it relentlessly. According to the rumours, he's bombed civilians, assassinated premiers and kidnapped wealthy individuals. He's dated a princess anonymously. Even became friends with the British Prime Minister once, just to prove he could do it. Always kept his identity secret though, just another anonymous face in the crowd. He's a killer, an intelligent madman who surrounds himself with highly capable security guards. And they're loyal to him, loyal as they can be. He treats those who perform well.'

'We've already been told he's gonna be hard to get close to,' Drake said.

'Practically impossible.'

'Oh, I could get close to him,' Alicia said. 'I'd have his little tail wagging in about five minutes.'

'That'll depend on what Crouch comes back with,' Drake told her, and then turned back to the phone. 'Anything else, guys?'

'He's careful, deadly, a ghost, a legend. The usual stuff. People I spoke to were telling me he'd always been just a rumour. Some kind of humorous spirit they made up to kill time and blame for mysterious events. A boogeyman, even.'

'Are there any pictures?' Mai asked.

'Good question,' Drake said. 'If we're gonna get close, we really need to know what he looks like.'

Cresswell broke that bubble. 'None whatsoever. We have no idea what he looks like.'

'That's not strictly true,' Anderson said. 'We got a few descriptions from the mercs, but you know what they're like. Nothing concrete or even matching.' He laughed without humour.

'Yeah, we've heard the descriptions,' Alicia said. 'Tall. Short. Bald, with a full head of hair.'

'What else can you tell us about him?' Kenzie asked.

'A bit of history,' Creswell said. 'As we mentioned, the tsar has been at this since he was young. The story told among his men goes like this. When he was a boy, his family mistreated him. And I mean all of them. His parents, brothers, sisters. The tsar was the runt of the litter.'

'How did you learn all this?' Hayden asked.

'Pieced it together from merc gossip,' Cresswell said. 'Anyway, one day our young tsar has had enough. He cracks. Stabs everyone and then torches the house with them in it. Ends up paying for his crimes despite what they did to him. While he's inside paying for his crimes, he learns a new way of life. Clings to it. Ends up loving it. He's finally found something he's good at. Just think... if his family hadn't mistreated him, there'd never have been a Dark Tsar.'

'No, there'd be someone else,' Drake said. 'Maybe someone worse. There always is.'

'The young tsar bettered himself in prison. Came out, joined a gang, soon moved through the ranks. Ended up in the top circle of some crime boss and then, when that crime boss wasn't paying attention, the tsar snatched away his kingdom. Grabbed it from him literally in one enormous chunk. He made sure the crime boss couldn't hit back and then started on his merry way. And... here we are.'

Drake listened in silence. The tsar's history wasn't unexpected. Many of these crime lords had strong-armed their way to the top. It came with the territory. They thanked Cresswell and Anderson and ended the call.

Stared at each other.

'We wait for Crouch,' Drake said.

'The timeline to the next bombing is getting closer,' Kenzie said, fretting.

'I know, but he has a lot of moving parts. He'll be

developing back stories for us, proof that we belong in a bad guy environment. He'll be setting up contacts we can use to prove we are who we say we are. Some kind of digital trail. Crouch is a professional. We're trusting him with our lives.'

'I hadn't quite looked at it that way,' Shaw said. Shaw didn't know Crouch as well as they did. 'I hope he's as good as you say he is.'

Alicia nodded. 'He'll come through.'

The team cooled their heels some more. Drake took several deep breaths. This wasn't what he was used to, what any of them were used to. He needed to be part of the action, to get involved and make a difference. The Dark Tsar needed taking down, and he knew his team was good enough to do it.

'Come on, Michael,' he said to himself. 'Make the call.'

CHAPTER TWENTY THREE

Days passed.

The team was ready. Crouch called them often, explaining what their individual roles would be, how they could make it all work. Drake didn't like the idea of splitting up – especially when they were going into the lion's den – but there was no other choice. They were headed once more into the heart of darkness, and they would live or die by their own decisions. And eventually, it would be kill or be killed.

The team split up and went back to their own houses. They showered and ate and did all the mundane things as they stood around waiting. The day turned around them, offering up heavy drizzle and then a hefty wind that battered the windows and howled through the eaves. There were long, dark nights in which they struggled to sleep. All this time, the Dark Tsar was reaching his goals as the Ghost Squadron cooled their heels.

Drake had a dream about being part of the tsar's envoy and having to watch the murderer kill a man just to stay undercover. He woke bathed in sweat and found it hard to get back to sleep again.

The next day dawned and still they waited on that final call to arms. Every minute that passed crushed them. Drake was sick of the waiting routine, as was

Alicia. They couldn't relax, struggled to sit down. It was all a waiting game.

And then, finally, Crouch called.

CHAPTER TWENTY FOUR

It started with Drake and Alicia. First, they were told by Crouch to expect a phone call. Next, the phone rang and a husky voice summoned them to Istanbul, where a special meeting would take place.

'Come as you are,' the voice said. 'No baggage. You will not need it if you are selected.'

Drake and Alicia said a quick goodbye to the rest of the team and then jumped on a plane to Istanbul. The flight was long and anxious. Obviously, Crouch's work had already held up. They'd been selected for the test and had been contacted out of the blue. It was a good sign.

Still, this was the quickest and hardest way to infiltrate the tsar's organisation. But, if successful, it would put them within striking distance of him.

The plane flew through interminable turbulence. Drake held on with white-knuckled hands. Even the cabin crew were forced to take their seats and, Drake knew, that was never a good sign. Seeing a flight attendant clutching the airs of their chairs as if their lives depended on it didn't exactly promote relaxation.

The plane bounced down in Istanbul with a squeal of tyres right on time, taxiing across the runway to the terminal. Soon, Drake and Alicia were through customs and, having no bags, found themselves quickly outside searching for a taxi. It was sweltering out here, a firm change from DC, forcing Drake to wipe his brow.

'Not used to this, love,' he said.

'Stop whining.'

They grabbed a taxi and reeled off the address. The guy looked surprised but said nothing. Soon, they were travelling along roads full of potholes and dodging civilians. The taxi drove them around the main town rather than straight through it, heading for an industrial area.

Drake checked the time. They were perfectly poised to make their appointment. He hated going in blind like this, unarmed, unprepared for what would happen, but he knew there was no choice. Finally, the car stopped, and the driver pointed out their address.

Drake gazed at it through the car window. A single storey warehouse clad in rectangular grey corrugations squatted a few dozen yards to the left, a gravel path leading up to a narrow side door. There was nobody around, but he saw several CCTV cameras.

They got out, and the car sped off, not wanting to hang around. Again, the heat hit them. Drake stared up at the startling blue skies. He walked with Alicia to the side door and knocked. He made sure the CCTV could see them both, standing easily, posing no threat.

Soon, the door opened, but no smiling face appeared. Instead, a gun pointed out at them, big and black and cocked.

'Who the fuck are you?' a gravelly voice growled.

'Alicia and Drake,' Alicia said. 'Here to see Javier.'

The gun stayed trained on them as Drake heard footsteps walk away. Minutes passed in uncomfortable silence. This time, the sweat stippling across Drake's forehead wasn't entirely to do with the heat.

Presently, the footsteps returned. The gun disappeared to be replaced by a face, a dark, grizzled face that looked like it had been out in the sun too long. When the man opened his mouth, he revealed a set of crooked yellow teeth.

'Javier will see you,' he said. 'Follow me.'

They stepped into the warehouse together, glad to get out of the direct sun. In silence, they traversed a long corridor with offices to each side and then went through another door to the warehouse proper. It was a vast, hangar-like space, almost empty. They crossed it, their boots echoing, until they came to another set of offices at the far side. Their guide pointed at a white door.

'Go through. Javier is waiting.'

Alicia opened the door first. Drake followed, finding himself in a small room with a white desk and three chairs. A kitchen unit stood at the far side, the kettle still steaming. A man sat facing them, sipping from a mug. He wore an expensive suit and gold jewellery. His eyes narrowed as he stared at them.

'You come well recommended,' he said in a nasally voice. 'Highly recommended, in fact. I checked and then checked again. Sit down.'

Drake nodded and did as he was asked. Alicia glared nonchalantly around the room for a few seconds before following suit. Javier sipped more of his drink.

'You're mercenaries out of Africa,' he said. 'Out of Syria, out of Iraq. You have gotten around. Always the best vacation places, yes?' he laughed at his own joke but didn't wait for a response. 'You have been very successful.'

'We're well trained, well-versed, experienced,' Drake said. 'Perfect for the job.'

'And why do you wish to switch to protection?'

Alicia shrugged. 'Sick of the dirt, the weather, the rough life. Never knowing where you'll be, what orders you'll follow, who you're killing. We want to work for someone who knows what they're doing and takes what they want.'

'You know who you'll be working for?'

'Sure.'

Javier studied them. 'And if I asked for a practical demonstration?'

Drake blinked. 'What would you like us to do?'

'Just the reply I was looking for. Now, stand up.'

They rose. They followed Javier out of the office. Outside, two big bruisers were waiting, cracking their knuckles. There were also two targets set up halfway across the warehouse. Javier's men threw two knives to the floor.

'I want you to incapacitate these men and then hit the targets in less than a minute. Don't kill them, don't break anything. Just take them out of the picture and then use your knives. Got it?'

Drake and Alicia nodded. The two big bruisers faced them, both leering. Drake faced his opponent. The man had huge arms covered in tattoos, a bald head, and dripped with sweat. When Javier said, 'Do it!' he started lumbering forward. Drake let him come. When the man was close, Drake kicked out at his knee, turning it sideways, and then sent a blow to the ribs, almost but not quite breaking them. Keeping with the pressure points, he slammed a fist into the guy's ears, and then sideswiped him in the throat. The big guy folded, holding his neck, panting, staring at the ground. Drake scooped up his knife and hit the target.

Alicia followed a similar pattern but was less subtle. At first, she didn't move at all, letting her opponent come uncomfortably close. Then, in true Alicia style, she booted him in the balls and lifted a knee into his swiftly descending face. The guy didn't cry out or groan so much as wheeze. But he didn't go down. He reached out for her, gripping her jacket. Alicia spun out of his grip and came around with a sidekick to the top of the head, stunning him. The man fell to his knees, shuddering, face down. Alicia reached out for her knife and threw it easily at the target, scoring a bullseye.

Both she and Drake turned to Javier.

The man was wincing, staring at the two downed bruisers with startled eyes. 'Well, you can certainly take people out at short notice,' he said. 'But what happens if you're surprised?'

They came from behind. Two short fast men wearing black leather jackets. In their hands they carried deadly knives. They lunged at Drake and Alicia.

Drake stepped away, twisted, saw the knife go by. He grabbed the arm and, reacting instantly and how he'd been trained, broke it at the wrist. You didn't mess with a knife wielder. The man screamed, dropped his knife, but then twisted, coming up with another knife in his left hand. This one was also thrust at Drake, but he was ready. He slammed a fist down onto the man's wrist, simultaneously kicking out and damaging a knee. Then he trapped the knife arm and delivered a crushing blow to the man's nose. Blood flew. The guy sagged, the second knife now dropping to the floor.

Alicia's opponent fared little better. He jumped at her, knife raised and slashing down at her head. She moved further under him, beyond the arc of the knife, shoved her shoulder into his midriff and threw him to the left. He tumbled messily, rolling fast. She leapt after him, treading on the knife arm and breaking it, then kicked him in the face and throat. The guy didn't even have time to reach for his second knife. He was out like a light.

Javier watched it all, an impressed look on his face. When it was over, he clapped softly. 'Well, you certainly know what you're doing. Impressive. I've never seen my men taken out so quickly. Though I told you not to harm them.'

'A man with a weapon should be treated seriously at all times,' Drake said. 'No fucking around.'

Javier nodded. 'Well, now I am in need of two more men for a while,' he said. 'Know anyone?' and again he laughed at his own joke, not expecting a reaction and not getting one. He studied Drake and Alicia. 'You are not even panting.'

Drake shrugged. 'We're good at what we do.'

'I see that. Do you know the kind of man my boss is?'

It was a question out of the blue. Drake wondered briefly how to tackle it. 'I know he's fair but ruthless, calm and decisive, brutal but content. He's also happy in his own way and content to share that with those he thinks deserve it.'

'And how do you know all that? My boss is supposed to be a mystery man.'

'You can't stop mercs gossiping,' Alicia said. 'They're better at it than combat. It's what they do best.'

'Really? I will have to remember that.'

'Mercs. Hookers. Party animals,' Drake said. 'They all talk. I'm amazed your boss has remained a ghost all this time.'

Now Javier smiled. 'Well, you said he was brutal,' he whispered shortly.

Drake understood the sentiment. He didn't answer, just stood his ground as the four men they'd taken out groaned close to their feet.

'You want to work for the Dark Tsar?' Javier said. 'I can arrange that. But once you're in, there's no backing out. You will stay for the duration of your tour.'

'Our tour?'

'That's what you call it, isn't that right? When you go away on a mission for months at a time. You call it a tour.'

Drake nodded. 'I know what you mean.'

'And will you gossip after you're done?'

Drake held a hand to his heart. 'Promise not to.'

It was a flippant comment, but what the hell else could he say? Javier would either believe him or he wouldn't.

'All right,' Javier said. 'You have the right credentials. You came highly recommended by people I trust. I've seen you in action. You've got the job.'

Inside, Drake rejoiced. On the outside, he remained icy. 'Thank you,' he managed.

Javier waved his hands, summoning men to him. Drake now saw guns from other offices had covered them and from on high. If they'd tried anything, they'd have been cut down in moments. Dake counted eight men and women emerging from concealment. He looked sideways at Javier. The man was clearly an important cog in the tsar's organisation.

'Do we report directly to you?' he fished.

'No, you report to a captain. But all that will be explained to you when you reach the tsar's residence. Are you ready to fly?'

'He doesn't live in Istanbul?'

'The journey won't be long. Come with me now. We will return home together.'

And Javier led the way out of the warehouse. Drake and Alicia managed a quick glance, a nod of recognition and satisfaction at what they'd achieved, before stepping into line. Thanks mostly to Crouch's background involvement and their own expertise, they had infiltrated the tsar's security.

They could only hope the others had similar success.

CHAPTER TWENTY FIVE

Torsten Dahl and Mano Kinimaka found they were called up almost as soon as Drake and Alicia departed. They barely had time to sip their fresh coffees before an email slipped into Kinimaka's inbox, asking for a meetup. It was so sudden, he almost choked on his coffee.

The big Hawaiian blinked at Dahl. 'We're up,' he said. 'Time to move.'

Dahl nodded, pleased. 'Where are we headed?'

Kinimaka rose to his feet. 'Bucharest.'

They said their goodbyes and headed out. For Dahl, it felt strange breaking the team up, saying goodbye. Mostly on missions, they stuck together. They worked better as a single entity. But this time, needs must.

They had to defeat the Dark Tsar by any means necessary. The team was out on a very shaky limb here, risking everything.

They made quick flight bookings and then good time to Bucharest. Neither of them was a nervy flyer, so they caught a good bit of sleep during the flight. The plane landed with a couple of hops and then they were through the airport and searching for a taxi. Kinimaka confirmed they had arrived, and within minutes, they were called to a meeting. A taxi drove them through the Romanian city to a built up district and dropped them off outside a cluster of highrise office buildings. Soon, they were pressing a buzzer and staring up at a CCTV camera.

'Appointment with Mr Carmichael,' Kinimaka said when someone answered. 'Dahl and Kinimaka here.'

The door clicked open. Dahl and Kinimaka squeezed through a narrow opening and then followed an equally narrow corridor. Soon, they pushed through a swing door to find themselves wedged into a very small office. A short man with thinning hair lounged behind a desk, leaning back, hands on his head.

Other than that, the place was empty.

'Sit down, sit down,' the man said.

The chairs were small and flimsy. Kinimaka perched on the end, worried that his might collapse beneath him. Dahl appeared to do the same.

'I expected more... security,' Dahl said quietly.

'Well, you are surrounded by armed guards in other rooms. The whole place is under constant surveillance. A rat couldn't get through here without getting its tail shot off. I think one man even has a bazooka. Does that help?'

Dahl nodded. 'Kind of.'

'Good, then let's get down to business. Someone I trust implicitly has forwarded your names to us. I'm told you're the best at what you do.'

Kinimaka inclined his head. 'Thank you.'

'Which is bizarre, because I thought we already employed the best,' the man shrugged. 'But never mind. There's almost someone better out there, I guess. But you want to work for the best and get paid accordingly? Am I right?'

This time, Dahl nodded. 'We're always looking for a new client.'

'You're going to have to prove to me you're worth it.' Now the man leaned forward, suddenly all business.

Dahl stared straight at him. 'Give us a challenge.'

The man narrowed his eyes. 'You can get anything, right? Anything I want at the drop of a hat? You're procurers, the best money can buy. At least, that's what I'm told. Let's accept that for a moment. Tell me... if you get this job, are you okay working for just one man, living in-house, available to him at any hour of the day?'

Dahl sat back. 'As you said – the pay should be worth it.'

'We're not just looking for people motivated by the green stuff. We want loyalty, conscientiousness, devotion. Can you bring that?'

'How long's the contract?' Kinimaka asked.

'Another interesting question without a definitive answer. My employer will have use of you...' he shrugged. 'Long term.'

'Is that the only way he does business?' Dahl tried to make their side of the conversation more believable and uncertain.

'He only uses the best, and on his terms.'

Dahl looked sideways at Kinimaka and gave the pretence of a nod. 'Then we will accept those terms.'

'Oh, it won't be that easy,' the short man said. 'First, I want a practical demonstration. And you will do it right here, in my office.'

Dahl made a face. 'What would you like us to do?'

'I thought about this long and hard. Some things

take time, I understand. For instance, if I asked for the new unobtainable Gucci timepiece with the diamond bracelet and gold bezel, it might take a few weeks. I accept that. But what I'm more interested in – and what my boss will be more interested in – is weapons. How are you with weapons?'

Dahl shrugged. 'Try us.'

'I intend to. Now, sit back and relax. I want you to procure me an RPG in Madrid. And I want it delivered with spare rockets in three hours. The clock starts now.' The short man made a point of looking at his watch.

Dahl raised an eyebrow, turned to Kinimaka, and gave him a lazy smile. 'Do you want to take this one, my friend, or shall I?'

'Happy to,' Kinimaka showed no sign of the nerves he was feeling and fished out his phone. He made a point of calling one number, answering a couple of identification question, and then calling another. He did this three times. Dahl nodded at the short man's questioning glance.

'It's all about security, secrecy, and previously known protocols,' he said. 'We stay alive and free that way.'

He received a nod in response. Kinimaka now called another number – which was actually the same number he'd been ringing all along – and connected to Michael Crouch's burner phone.

'Oh, Adrian,' he said, following an agreed protocol. The name 'Adrian' told Crouch that Kinimaka was finally getting down to business.

'Hello, my friend,' Crouch played along just in case someone was listening. 'What can I do for you today?'

'You are my man in Madrid, yes?'

'Madrid? Yes, I can do Madrid, though it is getting harder in that city these days.'

'Hard? For you? I will not hear it,' Kinimaka laughed loudly. 'Listen to what I need.' And the Hawaiian reeled off exactly what he wanted, wasting no time. Three hours, he knew, was definitely pushing it.

As expected, Crouch tried to keep his voice steady. 'Three hours?'

'You will be well compensated, my friend.'

'Give me an address.'

The short man, listening, held out a slip of paper. Kinimaka reeled it off to Crouch, who then asked if there was anything else required in a sarcastic voice.

'Are you sure you don't want a case of the best Russian vodka? A brace of strippers? A gaggle of hoodlums? Would you like a-'

'Three hours,' Kinimaka said and hung up.

The men were left staring at each other. To pass the time, the short man ordered someone to fetch them tea and coffee and bites to eat. Dahl and Kinimaka found themselves snacking and drinking with the enemy and resorting to small talk. After a while, they stood up and went for a walk, though still under the watchful eyes of their potential new employers.

Two hours and forty-five minutes later, Kinimaka's phone rang. He was sitting in the office, opposite the small man with Dahl alongside.

'It's done,' Crouch said.

At the same time, the short man's phone started to ring. He answered and listened for a few seconds, then hung up. He nodded slowly.

Kinimaka thanked Crouch and looked at the short man.

'Are we good?'

'I am sure you know we are.'

'RPG delivered?' Dahl made a satisfied face. 'And early.'

They both looked expectantly at the short man. He smiled without humour. 'You have got yourselves a job,' he said. 'Welcome to the dark heart of the tsar's organisation.'

'What happens next?' Dahl asked.

'You will be taken to the main house. From there, you will do your job. The tsar will have needed of you night and day and at a moment's notice. The job won't be easy, but it will be rewarding.'

Kinimaka sat back, both happy and nervous at completing his assignment. This would bring them into the very lair of the man they were seeking. He just hoped the others were having similar successes.

CHAPTER TWENTY SIX

Hayden, Kenzie, and Mai walked straight into the nightclub, bypassing the long line that stretched around the block. There were shouts of complaint, but they didn't slow. Their names were on the shortlist.

The bouncers gave them the cursory pat down and then they were let inside but, instead of heading towards the main area they were directed to a discreet set of stairs to the right. The stairs were hidden from the main area by a thick curtain and stretched upward for two floors. Hayden went first, the others following.

They'd been contacted just an hour after Dahl and Kinimaka. The email had dropped into the inbox, inviting them to J's nightclub on 9th Street NW that evening. At first, they were surprised, expecting to be asked to venture to some far-flung corner of the world. But then they shrugged and just took it in their stride. It wasn't beyond the bounds of possibility that the Dark Tsar would have trusted operatives working in DC.

Hayden wore a knee-length black dress and high heels. The others were attired similarly. They wore their hair down. They climbed the stairs together, wondering what was waiting for them at the top.

The noise of the nightclub assaulted their senses, banging music circulating around the dance floor and drowning out any conversation. Through gaps in the curtain, Hayden could see a horde of gyrating people, others standing and watching around the fringes, still more standing at the two bars and screaming to be heard. Men and women danced in cages here and there, others on small stages. The beat was a non-stop pounding pulse that set Hayden's teeth grinding.

She reached the top floor. Two men stood facing them, looking bored. These men wore jackets that clearly covered their handguns. When the women appeared, both men approached.

'Arms up,' one of them said.

'We've already been groped, thanks,' Kenzie said, nodding back down the stairs. 'back at the door.'

The men shrugged. They patted the women down lightly and then knocked at a door. Hayden heard a voice bark a question. One man stuck his head through the door and then beckoned to Hayden. Soon, the three women were standing inside a cramped little room. Facing them was a bearded, well-built man wearing a tight T-shirt and sitting behind a messy desk. The man looked hassled.

'You can call me Jack,' he said, and then flipped open a folder on his desk. 'I'm guessing you are Hayden, Kenzie and Mai?'

They nodded, standing uncomfortably side by side. There was nowhere to sit or even move in the tiny office. The man behind the desk blinked at them.

'Right, well, you sure look the part. I've been told you're the very best though and that we should retain your services. What else can you do?'

'You know why we're here,' Hayden said. 'We're entertainers. We look the part, we can professionally pour, mix, serve and even drink the drinks. We can dance, be discreet, be loud, grab attention. We can mingle, make conversation, smooth out issues. But we're not here for anything sleezy. You want professional, you got professional. Don't try any dirty tricks.'

The man grinned at them, beard waggling. 'I hear you. I know you're not here to dance naked, more's the pity. But what can you do?'

'I just told you,' Hayden said. 'We're the best at what we do.'

'The boss has a twenty-four-hour party going on at his house. Sometimes he's there, sometimes not. He needs a lot of attention when he's in a partying mood. We provide him with the very best people capable of doing that. It's a great responsibility. You would be well compensated for it. People tell me you're the best.'

'Put us in the right position and we'll excel,' Kenzie said.

'And you?' The man looked at Mai. 'What are you good at?'

'I can kick proper ass,' she said. 'If it comes to it.'

The man's eyes widened. 'Ah, so you provide bodyguard service as well?'

'If it becomes necessary,' Hayden said.

'Is there anything you can't do?' he smiled.

'Just keep it professional. That way, we all know where we stand. We're entertainers by trade. That means we offer a professional service and look good doing it. We serve drinks, pass through the crowd, dance, take orders, handle disputes, break up fights, hit back if we have to. We run the bar area, manage it, keep everything running smoothly. Identify the rotten apples, weed them out.'

'How do I know you're as good as you say you are?'

'You have our recommendations. Yeah, we could start working downstairs in the bar, but it's not something you can show in just a few minutes, or a couple of hours. It takes a bit of time to effectively stage manage the whole entertainment role.'

The bearded man sat back, reached into a nearby filing cabinet and pulled out a half empty bottle of whisky. He poured himself a couple of shots, then held the bottle out to them.

'Want some?'

'We don't drink on the job unless we're told to by the boss.'

Jack nodded and threw his whisky back. 'Good. Do you know who you will be working for?'

'Of course. Our contacts are every bit as good as yours.'

Lack raised his eyebrows as if surprised to hear that. 'And you will be okay working permanently in-house?'

'It will work for us for a while.'

'If you are as good as you say you are, the boss will not want to lose you.'

Hayden shrugged. 'The stay is negotiable. '

Jack looked longingly at all three of them. Hayden knew they had him hook, line and sinker. She gave him her best smile.

'Do you want us?'

'Yeah, we have other offers,' Mai added.

Jack rose quickly to his feet. 'How soon can you be ready to fly?'

Hayden made a point of looking surprised. 'Fly? To where?'

'That's classified,' Jack tried to look important. 'But it's a long-haul flight.'

Hayden looked across to Kenzie and Mai and tried not to smile too broadly. 'We're ready when you are, Jack. Are you coming with us?'

Jack gulped. 'I wish,' he said. 'No. You'll be directed on what to do, where to go. The flight will be on a private plane.'

Hayden nodded. 'For security, I get it. Well, the rest is up to you, Jack. Do you want us?'

'Oh, I want you. And I'm sure the boss will too. How are you at fending off advances in a professional manner?'

Mai shrugged. 'Try me.'

Jack looked at her with a little trepidation. 'Maybe I'll take your word for it,' he said. 'But I have to warn you. The boss can be pretty intense.'

'We can handle intense,' Kenzie said.

Jack shrugged. 'If you say so.'

'What happens next?' Hayden asked.

'Just wait there. I'll get it all organised for you. Shouldn't take long.' And Jack reached out his hand to pick up the phone.

CHAPTER TWENTY SEVEN

Cam and Shaw waited the longest. It was decided that they should go in as special thieves and, to keep the attention as far away from Crouch's involvement as possible, they didn't use Michael. They used an alternative route.

Through the years, Cam, being a thief and a fighter most of his life until he met Alicia, had made a slew of contacts of his own. One of them was as close to the Dark Tsar as it was likely to get. Cam reached out and asked her to get Shaw and him an audience. The woman agreed and made the calls, but it took longer than Cam had expected. They were stuck in DC for hours after the others departed.

Finally, though, a call came through. Cam answered in a hurry. 'Do you have it?'

The woman, his contact, was named Nicola. She said, 'You're thieves. The best. I've vouched for you. Cam, are you sure about this? The Dark Tsar is one of the worst dudes in the world.'

Cam assured her he was and needed the money. That, at least, she could understand. She went on. 'Through my connections, I got you an audience. It's a top class job. Getting you close to the Tsar himself. I hope to God you're still as good as you used to be during your carnival days. They'll test you, you know.'

Cam grasped the phone tighter. 'I've lost nothing,' he lied. 'And I've kept my hand in.'

'I hope so. But listen, travel to Ankara in Turkey. You have a meeting arranged with a man named Binici. Don't be late.' She reeled off a time and place.

Shaw jumped into action, booking them the earliest flights to Turkey, making sure they would arrive in ample time for their meeting tomorrow. Cam signed off with Nicola, feeling anxious. He wasn't, by any stretch of the imagination, a superb thief. He was competent because he'd had to be, but he wasn't any better than your every day, run-of-the-mill burglar. If they were tested hard, he feared the outcome.

But Shaw was good at what she did. Cam had no doubt that, together, they would succeed.

They travelled to the airport in a taxi, waited around for boarding, and then settled back as it took off. Hours passed. The flight to Turkey was a long one, and both of them grabbed some sleep, entirely missing the in-flight meals. By the time they landed, they were both starving, and it was late morning of the day of their meeting. Cam checked his watch as they waited at security.

'Seven hours,' he said. 'Plenty of time.'

They went immediately to their hotel and booked in, then went for a meal. Not a lot of conversation passed between them. They were both anxious, wondering what was to come. Cam didn't like to be without the blanket security provided by the entire team acting as a unit, but sometimes, this was the drill. If they wanted to stop any more bombings, this was what they had to do.

They killed some time in their room, checked the address of the meeting on Google Maps and saw that it was a fifteen-minute walk away. All good. Cam wanted to check in with Alicia, but knew by now she'd be undercover, just as he and Cam were trying to be. They were all on their own now.

The time approached. They left the hotel, feeling a dark chill in the air. Cam turned the collar of his jacket up, wishing he'd worn something warmer. But there had been no time to pack, no time to choose clothes. This was all a whirlwind of action.

They reached their destination: a warehouse with a big roller shutter door to the left, a narrow normal door to the right. Cam tapped at the normal door, rapping on the glass.

Almost immediately, the roller shutter started to rattle upwards. Cam saw boots, legs, and then the torso of a short man with wide, muscly shoulders and a thick head of hair. He looked like a bulldog with his broad chest and short legs and the way he glared at them with his scrunched-up face.

'This better be good. What do you want?'

As he spoke, several figures materialised out of the darkness behind him. Cam saw seven men, all carrying an assortment of weapons. The men were hard-faced and flinty eyed. He nodded at the bulldog.

'Cam and Shaw,' he said easily. 'We have an appointment. Told to ask for a man named Binici.'

The harsh gaze eased a little. 'I am Binici. You are the best thieves in the world, apparently.'

Cam winced inwardly. 'We do our best,' he said.

'And modest too,' Binici growled, his Turkish accent as thick as syrup. 'Come inside. You don't know how many eyes the night has.'

They followed him into the warehouse and blinked as someone threw on a load of lights. The place was packed with machinery, boxes, and old cars. There were kitchen units along one side with a plastic table and sets of chairs and it was towards these that Binici led them.

'Someone I trust very much has told me you are the best at what you do,' Binici said as they walked. 'They insisted I meet you. Said you might prove very valuable to our organisation.'

As he spoke Binici didn't meet their eyes, just walked with his eyes on the floor. The other men shadowed them, weapons still close to hand, giving Cam an itchy feeling down the centre of his back.

He didn't like this setup at all.

'We know many people,' Shaw said. 'We've done some world class jobs.'

'Can you name some of them?'

'That would be unprofessional,' Cam said. 'Suffice to say: the three diamond job in Helsinki, the Rolex haul in Los Angeles, the Faberge egg in Tokyo. I won't say that was us, but...' he fell silent.

'I thought I knew who did the Helsinki job.' Binici frowned. 'I must be mistaken.'

Cam bit the inside of his mouth. It had been a risk, and Binici was clearly well connected. But he thought he'd got away with it. At his side, Shaw cleared her throat, an unspoken signal to keep the words to a minimum.

'Are you planners or pantsers?' Binici asked.

Cam knew the best answer to that. 'Planners,' he said. 'We take our time, but we cover all angles.'

'That's a shame,' Binici said. 'I was hoping I could

order you to fetch me something hot and expensive tonight.'

Cam had been expecting that, too. He said, 'Give us the right environment to work in, some time, and let us plan. That's how we work best, and the only terms we'll work too.'

Binici looked surprised. 'You won't steal quickly to order?'

Cam shrugged. 'Nothing's impossible. But we'd prefer not to.'

Binici filled the kettle and flicked it on. 'Tea?'

'No thanks.' Shaw also shook her head.

'So how are we supposed to test you?' Binici asked. 'I can't just let you into the inner circle without knowing you're the elite.'

Cam held out his hands. 'You have our references.'

Binici laughed. 'Yes, and they're good. But it's my bollocks if you turn out to be a pair of useless assholes, if you know what I mean.'

Cam said nothing. Both he and Shaw waited for Binici to come to some decision. 'You know this is an in-house job? You will get personal access to the boss and must steal anything he asks for. Can you do that?'

'I think we're good enough,' Shaw said.

'You'd better do better than 'think',' Binici said. 'If you fail the boss, you won't last long.' At this, there were some sniggers from the men gathered around.

Binici brewed himself a tea and sat back with the steaming mug in his hand. He gazed speculatively at Cam and Shaw. Cam knew that they'd be ordered to commit some crime, to prove they were as good as they were touted to be.

And then Binici surprised him.

'I'm gonna go with my gut,' he said. 'And believe in my connections. *They* say you're the best. I'm gonna go with that. You're in. How do you feel about that?'

Cam smiled widely but, inside, he wasn't so sure. It had been easy... too goddamn easy. As an ex-fighter, ex-thief and fairground worker, he knew that life wasn't easy. Nothing came without a trial.

Except this, it seemed.

He glanced surreptitiously at Shaw. He knew her. Though her expression was blank, he knew she was fighting hard to keep the look of shock off her face.

What was going on?

Binici finished his tea with a quick swig and then rose to his feet. 'I need an answer from you.'

Cam nodded. 'Sure. I just expected it to be harder, that's all.'

'Ah, but now you're right where I want you. At my side. Soon, you'll be at the Tsar's side. Are you sure you're up to the task?'

Cam was barely following Binici's words. He was worried, his heart pounding. They had exactly what they wanted... but it had been far too easy.

'We can get anything he asks for,' Shaw said.

'I'll hold you to that,' Binici told them with finality.

CHAPTER TWENTY EIGHT

'It's your lucky day,' Javier said to Drake as the two of them sat close to each other on the private jet. Javier had wasted no time jumping on the plane with his cohorts and starting on the journey to the tsar's home. An hour in, though, he had received a phone call.

Drake glanced at Alicia in the seat beside him and then regarded Javier. 'It is?'

'You can prove your worth right away. There's a job needs doing.'

Drake cursed inwardly. Why was nothing ever easy? All they wanted was to get to the tsar's home, meet up with the others if they'd made the cut, and then handle the tsar himself. 'Before we arrive?' he asked.

Javier shrugged. 'Straight away. We're headed for Turkey. When we land, we'll go straight to the arms deal. You're added protection.'

'Arms deal?'

'You have to get used to taking orders without asking questions. But, since you're here, and we have time, I'll tell you. There's an arms deal going down, oh in about an hour, and the boys would benefit from a little extra protection. That's us three. You can handle that, right?' He was grinning as he asked the question.

'Right place at the right time,' Drake said. 'You couldn't write it.'

'Trouble is, it's a new arms dealer,' Javier went on. 'First deal. We recently lost a man named Soroyan, who was our primary dealer.'

'You have?' Alicia said. 'That's a shame.'

Javier shrugged. 'That's the game, I'm afraid. You have to adapt constantly. Fortunately, the tsar's good at adapting and so am I. When we land, be ready to move fast.'

Drake looked out the window. The day had got away from them and darkness had fallen. By the time the plane touched down, it was pitch black.

They were whisked through the airport to several waiting cars. In the back, they were handed surreptitious weapons – handguns – and told to keep them concealed. Javier gave them a few spare mags for their pockets.

'Are we expecting trouble?' Drake asked.

'We aren't expecting anything,' Javier said. 'This is a first deal. Shit happens. Be ready. Let's call this your audition.'

The cars raced to their destination, caring little for speed limits or slower vehicles. The night was dark and drizzly, a stiff wind rocked the car. Drake and Alicia sat in silence, surrounded by darkness.

Soon, the cars pulled up outside a ratty-looking warehouse. Drake noticed there was already a line of vehicles parked at the kerb. When Javier's car pulled up, doors started to open. Soon, the pavement was filled with hard looking men and women. Drake counted an even dozen, including Javier. The man in charge approached Javier deferentially.

'Didn't know you were coming, sir. Do you want to take over?'

'Last minute request. No, I'm happy for you to handle the deal, Agha.'

The man turned and gave an order, speaking in Turkish and English. Together, they all started walking towards the warehouse. As they approached, the roller shutter doors opened. Drake kept his hand near his gun, prepared for anything.

A man stepped out of the warehouse. His hair was long and grey, his face lined with age. Men in suits surrounded him, their hands hovering close to their midriffs. A wave of tension passed from those inside to those outside, curdling the air.

Agha stepped forward and held out a hand. 'Mr Belson. It is good to finally meet you.'

The older man shook briefly. 'I rarely attend these meetings.'

Meaning, Drake thought, this guy was the big boss. He thought such things were below him. But, for the tsar, he had made an exception. Drake kept a close eye on all the muscle surrounding Belson, counted eight men and three women, all poised and ready to act. His eyes probed the surrounding shadows and the depths of the warehouse too, seeking threats. Nothing moved.

'Let's get this over with quickly,' Belson said.

He stepped back inside the warehouse. Agha and his contingent followed. Someone snapped some lights on and then closed the roller shutter door. Drake listened as it clattered down behind them. They were standing in a dusty warehouse, surrounded by crates. Benson pointed to the nearest one.

'Sidearms,' he said. 'All Beretta M9s. Powerful weapon. That crate there is full of M67 fragmentation grenades. One over is M9s,' he spread his hands. 'Poor reputation, I know, but it's not like you're planning to use them. You're just the middlemen,' he went on, labelling each crate and finally turning to look Agha in the eye. 'My money?'

Agha pointed at two random crates. Men grabbed crowbars and walked over to lift the lids and inspect the contents. A few minutes passed. Drake stayed in silence with Alicia at his side, both of them close to cover and with their hands steady, just inches from their weapons. Javier was to their right, carefully assessing the situation.

Soon, the men nodded at Agha. Belson looked aggrieved, as if upset they hadn't simply taken his word for it. Now he looked at Agha with more intensity. 'The payment?'

Agha clicked his fingers. Someone brought a laptop and laid it on top of a crate. Agha started clicking buttons, finally turning the screen around so that Belson could see it.

'Just needs your account details,' he said.

Belson entered them quickly and then nodded in satisfaction. A wide smile settled across his lined face. 'And that's how we do business,' he said.

Drake saw them first. Shadows in the rafters above their heads. They were slinking forward, moving slowly as if testing the weight of the beams. But that wasn't it at all. These shadows held guns.

'Heads up!' he shouted, and reached for his weapon.

At his side, Alicia ducked for cover as she pulled

out her gun. Javier heard and did the same. Agha stared up, goggling. Drake now saw four shadows up there, all with their guns pointed down. Belson and his goons were melting backwards.

A shot rang out from above. One of Agha's men went down, shot through the heart. More shots filled the warehouse, slamming down among Agha's people. Drake had already lined one of the figures up. He fired. The shape flinched and then dropped its weapon before losing its grip on the beam and tumbling to the floor. Beside him, Alicia fired and hit her target.

Now, Belson's people reached for their own weapons. Agha shouted a warning, whipped out his own gun, and fired first. Suddenly, bullets were flying across the warehouse between the two contingents, searing the air. Belson had flung himself to the ground, a manic grin on his face. The warehouse resounded with the sound of gunfire.

Drake crouched behind his crate, still seeing those above as the greatest threat. They were firing constantly, taking out Agha's men. Drake lined another one up, knowing they couldn't exactly take cover. He squeezed his trigger, brought another man down. Beside him, Javier had also sensed the greatest threat and now fired into the fourth and last shadow. This man also dropped like a stone, landing on top of a crate, coating it with blood.

Drake turned his attention to Belson's group. They were scattered behind the crates and a few oil drums. He waited, lining up one of the crates and, when a head popped out, blew it off. Beside him, Javier nodded appreciatively.

'I like your style.'

Drake turned to him. 'Is this usually how your arms deals go?'

'Are you kidding? When we used to use Soroyan, it all ran smooth as silk.'

Drake tried not to feel guilty about that. His team had taken Soroyan out of the game, at least temporarily, but Javier didn't need to know that. He half expected Alicia to come back with the innocent phrase 'What happened to Soroyan?' but, for now, saw she was concentrating on her enemy.

Bullets flew. Men and women were tagged, falling backwards. Drake counted four dead on their side, but more on Belson's. Figures were running between crates, getting closer to each other. He stayed put, not wanting to risk a stray bullet. It was Alicia who saw Belson crawling away just a few metres from them.

'If we get him, this is over,' she said.

Drake nodded.

Without further word, Alicia shouted 'Cover me!' and leapt out of hiding. Drake swore and leapt to her aid, laying down a hail of cover fire above her head. Javier did the same. Alicia crawled double-time to Belson, grabbed the man by the belt buckle and hauled him back. He half rose, realised there were bullets flying over his head, and then ducked back down. Alicia punched him in the kidneys.

'Get off me,' he cried. 'Help!'

But Drake and Javier's wall of lead kept their enemy under cover. Alicia dragged on Belson, pulling him with her as she returned to the cover of the crate. When she arrived, she yanked the man along with her, muscles straining. Belson waved and screamed and tried to attract the attention of his own people.

But Alicia had him. She punched him in the throat and then took a breather, sweat pouring from her forehead. She looked at Drake.

'Bell end,' he told her.

She shrugged. 'It was worth it, wasn't it?'

'You took an enormous risk.'

Javier leaned towards them. 'Great effort,' he said. 'I'd applaud you if I didn't need my hand for shooting these goons.'

They turned their attention to Belson. 'Traitorous prick,' Javier said. 'Call your men off or I'll shoot you in the throat.'

Belson's eyes were wide. He nodded, mouth opening with no sound coming out. Javier waved his gun before the man's eyes.

'Do it now!'

Belson, looking terrified, rose and opened his mouth. 'Stop!' He cried out. 'Stop firing! We need to-'

The man's head exploded in a cloud of red.

Drake gawped as the boss flew backwards, very dead. One of his people had shot him, not realising who he was. Drake stared at Javier. 'That turned out to be a bad idea.'

Javier was goggling at the dead boss. 'Shit,' he said.

'What the hell do we do now?' Alicia said. 'They don't know he's dead.'

'Or that they shot him,' Drake said. 'They'll think it was us.'

'Shit,' Javier repeated.

All around them, the gunfire continued. Five of Aghas and Javier's people were now dead. Bullets slammed into crates. Drake looked over, saw the crate of grenades and then looked at Alicia.

'You wanna do something crazy?'

'Every damn day.'

'Follow me.'

They raced out of cover. They didn't ask Javier to follow them, but he stuck close, seemingly not wanting to be left behind. Drake passed between crates until he reached the one that held the grenades, noting that the top was still half-off. He ducked behind it as a salvo of bullets smashed all around him.

Alicia changed mags. She nodded at Drake, reading his mind. He gave her a smile. 'Dahl would be proud,' he said.

And he rose, reached into the crate and scooped out an armful of grenades. Next, he started throwing them, aiming for their enemy's hiding places. Grenades looped through the air. When he was done, Drake ducked behind the crate.

'Duck the fuck down,' he said.

Seconds later, there was an ear-splitting roar. Drake covered his ears. Explosions rocked the warehouse. He heard groaning timbers and beams and the sounds of screaming men. A wave of hot air rushed past them. All around, he could hear shrapnel striking crates and oil drums and walls. The sound was so loud it hurt his brain.

When the percussive explosions were over, Drake tentatively raised his head, gun ready. The other side of the warehouse was a war zone, littered with spars of wood, bent metal, and dead bodies. Slowly, Agha's people started emerging from cover, many of them with bewildered expressions on their faces.

At his side, Javier cheered. 'Good job,' he said, waving his gun. 'Now we have the weapons.'

'Although you will have to get yourself a new arms dealer,' Alicia said flatly.

'That is unfortunate, but the tsar doesn't take double cross lightly. We only did what he would have ordered us to do.' he turned to Drake and Alicia. 'You two have turned out to be valuable assets.'

'Thanks,' Drake said. 'I think.'

'Just doing our job,' Alicia said.

Javier made a gesture to his remaining men and women. 'Let's pack this shit up and get the hell out of here.'

CHAPTER TWENTY NINE

It all happened quickly after that. Trucks had arrived. The weapons were loaded and taken away, the dead bodies left alongside the warehouse's walls. Once the job was done, Drake and Alicia were directed back to the cars, where they once again took their places in the back seat.

Javier jumped into the front, turned and handed them something. Drake was surprised to see they were blindfolds. Javier shrugged at their surprised expressions. 'Nobody knows where the tsar lives,' he said. 'Not right away.'

They endured a long journey in darkness, the twists and turns of the car making Drake feel nauseous. To him, it felt as if they were heading upward to some higher elevation, following a hilly road. Time passed, and he had no idea where they really were.

When they arrived, the blindfolds were removed. Drake climbed out of the car to a surprise. They were standing in a gravelly courtyard surrounded by the walls of a castle. Crenelated walls stretched to all sides and there were two towers and a tall keep. The walls looked cold and bleak. There were lights shining through various windows, and to the left, three modern garages. Other cars were parked around, and there were two men at the main doors. Drake was reminded that the tsar loved his partying and carousing.

He and Alicia waited to see what would happen next. Javier nodded at them and walked away. Soon, they were approached by Agha.

'You're the new guys,' he said. 'Follow me.'

Drake and Alicia exchanged a glance, but said nothing. They followed Agha towards the front doors, up some steps and then went through into the castle. They found themselves in a wide entranceway with a set of winding stairs to the left and several entrances. Agha led them to the right.

'Staff this way,' he said.

They followed him down several passageways, passing running waiters and two chefs and seeing several armed guards. They passed open rooms where guards sat eating, where waiting staff took breaks, where guards were exchanging their weapons as they went off shift. Drake and Alicia got a bird's-eye view of the Dark Tsar's kingdom, of how it worked, of the amount of people involved. They followed Agha without question through the twisting passageways of the castle.

All the time, Drake was looking out for his team.

So far, he'd seen nobody that he knew. But the others would have made it, he was sure. They were all at the very top of their game.

Agha led them to an office where a man sat waiting. Drake remembered that the deadline for the next bombing was edging closer and closer. He knew they had to end this as soon as possible, and that every wasted minute was a death knell.

Agha left them. The man behind the desk took their details and assigned them a room, gave them a map to show them exactly where it was. The map was marked with room numbers and bars and mess halls. The man asked if they were hungry, since their first shift wouldn't start until tomorrow. Drake saw that as a good opportunity to nose around and see whoever else was around and said yes, they were. Soon, they were looking for the mess hall. They passed lots of people in the hallways, all headed in different directions.

'It's a full on resort,' Alicia said quietly as they walked. 'There must be dozens of guards and then servers, chefs and butlers.'

'And don't forget the partygoers upstairs,' Drake said. 'Clearly, the tsar hides his real identity from all these people. I bet it's just the chosen few who know who he really is.'

'Or the money's really good,' Alicia said with a chuckle.

They followed the map, taking in more than just the way to the mess hall. It was a comprehensive diagram of the entire castle, with everything marked, including entrances and exits, windows and doors. It included the upstairs level, with rooms such as the Diamond Room, the Blue Room, and Private rooms marked. Drake and Alicia took it all in. Soon, they were standing in the doorway of the mess hall.

Drake took a few moments to check it out before they entered. It was a large space, the main part of it taken up with round tables and chairs. One side was a long buffet with hot and cold choices and drinks machines and coffee and tea areas. People queued along it with paper plates in their hands, waiting in line. Groups of men and women lined the sides of the room, eating while standing, where dozens of others sat at the tables. There was the loud din of conversation and laughter.

'All seem happy enough,' Alicia said.

Drake studied the faces, looking for certain people in particular. So far, he was drawing a blank.

'Wanna eat?' he asked.

'Fuck, yeah, I'm starving.'

They joined the buffet queue and filled their plates, then grabbed drinks and found a table. Soon, they were eating well and feeling much better. Drake never stopped studying the surrounding faces. He could tell Alicia wanted to talk, wanted to discuss what had happened so far, but there was no opportunity. They couldn't risk being overheard.

They took their time, figuring the mess hall was the busiest place in the castle and the place that their team would most frequent. Of course, they couldn't hope to see everyone here, but a couple would be nice. Both Drake and Alicia went up for seconds.

Drake checked the map again. 'There's a big bar area too,' he said. 'For off duty guards, I'm guessing. We should check that out.'

'Maybe split up?' Alicia asked.

'Maybe. Time is against us.'

They continued to eat and drink, taking their time. Drake took the measure of the assorted diners, especially the guards. So far, all their energy had been focused on getting inside the tsar's private domain. Now they were here, there was no coherent plan. Only that they had to stop the madman before he committed any more atrocities. Drake saw men who thought they were tough, men who were half-tough, and proper ex-special forces guys. He saw women who knew exactly how to handle themselves. When you were ex-army yourself, you tended to recognise the attributes. He pointed a few of them out to Alicia, especially the ones that might cause problems.

'What's the next step?' She asked.

'Find out who else is with us,' Drake said. 'But only for a short period. Tomorrow, we have a shift, whatever that entails. Maybe we'll get close to the tsar.'

They spoke in whispers, under their breath. Drake was nearing the end of his meal. They'd drawn this out as long as they could. He wondered if he should go top up his coffee again or head for the bar.

But he didn't think, in the circumstances, any of the team would be hanging out at the bar.

If they were here, maybe they just couldn't get away at the moment. Maybe they'd caught an immediate shift.

He looked at Alicia. 'Looks like we've-'

Her eyes widened. She didn't point, but Drake could tell she'd latched on to something. Could it be the tsar? Right here, right now...

Drake casually followed her eyeline. What he saw made him smile. Not too broadly, but he couldn't help a slight grin.

Dahl and Kinimaka were just joining the buffet queue. Drake remembered they were here as procurers. They were using Michael Crouch's connections to get anything to anywhere as fast as possible, a service that might well prove invaluable to the tsar. It seemed they had passed through the screening process.

Both Dahl and Kinimaka were scanning the crowd carefully, surreptitiously. They held paper plates in their hands, making them look slightly silly. Drake couldn't help but smile. As he did, he noticed the Swede's eyes latch on to him.

A slight nod. Dahl then nudged Kinimaka. The Hawaiians' greeting was more obvious, but still furtive enough. Drake and Alicia nodded back. This was as close as they would get. They couldn't risk being seen together.

Alicia turned to Drake. 'They made it.'

He kept his voice pitched as low as possible. 'I wonder how the others are getting on?' He especially wondered about Cam and Shaw, who had been using a different set of connections.

'I think we've hung out here as long as we can,' Drake said finally. By now, Dahl and Kinimaka had taken their seats and were eating their meals. Drake wished there was a way for them to communicate. Previously, they'd always been able to, but now there was no chance. They just couldn't risk any contact.

He rose to his feet. 'We'd best get some sleep,' he said. 'We don't know what to expect tomorrow.'

'Sleep?' Alicia repeated. 'In here? With all this danger? I don't think I'll sleep until I'm outta this place.'

Drake knew what she meant. They were well and truly out of their comfort zone, which, lately, had become DC. Maybe he was getting soft, losing it, but he hated the fact that they were far behind enemy lines, in dire territory. And he sure as hell wasn't used to going undercover.

'Maybe we'll sleep in shifts,' he said.

CHAPTER THIRTY

The next morning, Drake and Alicia reported for duty. This was achieved by approaching a man behind a desk, giving him their names, and then waiting to be handed their assignments. Apparently, they'd been chosen to guard the entertainment venue for the day.

Not understanding what that was, they followed directions.

They ended up in what Drake could only describe as an enormous nightclub without the loud, banging music. The place was a huge cavern at the centre of the castle, with muted lighting and spotlights whirling in several corners, with plush sofas and beanbags everywhere, a sumptuous carpet and tiled walls for soundproofing. Offices lined the walls, their glass windows looking out over the action. There were two dancefloors and two stages. There were coffee tables and poser tables everywhere. Drake remembered the tsar held a twenty-four-hour party in his castle and, today, it looked like he and Alicia were a major part of the honour guard.

'Shit,' Alicia said, looking around. 'Are you kidding me?'

He shared the sentiment. 'What are we actually supposed to do? Look out for drunks?'

'Yeah, I doubt there's a lot of trouble in here.'

'Eight hours of this,' Drake growled. 'Wonderful.'

As if to counterpoint his misery, a happy, upbeat dance tune broke out over the speakers, not overly loud. Drake grumbled something about 'bring on the Dinorock' and started moving through the crowd. Almost immediately, he sensed a presence at his side.

'You're new here, right?' An American accent rang in his ear.

Drake turned, saw a set of muscled shoulders and looked up at an extremely tall man. The guy was grinning, his mouth open to show a set of startingly white teeth.

'Yeah, thrown in at the bloody deep end.'

'They like to do that. And I bet they haven't even told you what to do.'

Drake gestured at the scattered crowd. 'Keep the peace, I guess.'

'I'm Quigley,' he held out a hand and shook both of theirs. 'Been at this for six months now.'

'Wow, you're a vet.'

'It sure feels that way. And you're right. You're here to make sure nobody does anything stupid. Some of the clientele... well, they're not your average joe.'

Drake saw a chance to fish. 'Friends of the tsar?'

'Special friends. You really have to keep a sharp eye on some of them and then act all diplomatically when they get out of line.'

'Wouldn't it be easier to just fuck them up a bit?' Alicia said.

Quigley laughed. 'Believe me, I want to. Some of them are absolute assholes.'

'Speaking of the tsar,' Drake went on. 'Isn't he usually around?'

Quigley nodded. 'You see that office over there?' He pointed to a prominent set of offices on the far side of the room. At the moment, some plush black curtains were drawn. 'That's his place. When the curtains are open, he's here.'

A good signal, Drake thought. He could work with that. 'Does he get involved? You know... mingle?'

Quigley laughed, not at all bothered by the line of questioning. 'The tsar loves to mingle,' he said. 'Especially with the ladies.' He cast a furtive glance at Alicia. 'You're his type, by the way.'

Alicia raised her eyebrows at that. 'His type? What do you mean by that?'

'Careful,' Drake said.

Quigley took a moment to choose the right words. 'Beautiful. Healthy. Capable. Intelligent,' he said. 'Are you gonna hit me?'

Alicia smiled graciously. 'No. I'll let it slide this once.'

'Thank you. Well, just wander. Keep to the edges and the shadows, mostly. We're supposed to stay subtle. Watch for trouble brewing. When it does, move in quickly and handle it carefully. I've seen punches thrown here, but nothing worse.'

Alicia gave him a 'challenge accepted' look and said, 'Who's in charge out here?'

Quigley nodded to the far corner. 'Couple of guys over there. Not important. You're left to your own devices. You only find out who's in charge if you fuck up.'

Drake thought a new line of questioning might

work. 'Does the tsar appear at a certain time?'

Now Quigley frowned at him. 'Why do you ask? Do you wanna meet him?'

Drake shrugged. 'The guy's famous,' he said in a non-committal way.

'Evenings,' Quigley said. 'Usually stays late. You're on the wrong shift.' He laughed.

'So...' Alicia said. 'Here's one for you. Are the staff allowed in here on their time off? Or do we have our own party room?'

'Good question,' Quigley said. 'Sometimes, yeah. It depends what you look like, who likes you, and who the guys on the door are. It's pot luck.'

'But you're gold if you get in here,' Alicia said. 'The mingling opportunities are endless.'

Quigley looked at her speculatively. 'I guess so. Do you have something in mind?'

Alicia laughed it off. 'No, of course not. Just an observation. Thanks for all your help.'

It was a subtle brush off, but it worked. Quigley grinned at them and moved off, glad he'd done his good deed for the day. Drake looked at Alicia.

'It's all fallen a bit flat.'

The Englishwoman looked at the drawn curtains on the other side of the room. 'So it seems. I guess we just do our jobs for now.'

They mingled. They patrolled the perimeter of the entire room several times, getting a feel for the place. At this time, it was relatively quiet, people sitting on the sofas and perched at the bars, standing in corners and talking. A bunch of guys in suits were seated near the middle, hunched forward and engaged in quiet conversation. Maybe a deal was being made.

Nothing good, Drake was sure. There was nobody on the dance floor, nobody around the poles and cages, nobody in any of the offices. But the guards were present. Drake counted eight of them, including him and Alicia and Quigley. They didn't exactly look bored, but they weren't active either. Most of them stood leaning against the walls, in repose. It took Drake and Alicia just an hour to fully reconnoitre the place. In that time, there was no sign of the tsar nor of anyone else they knew. They soon became bored.

Hours passed. Morning became afternoon. As lunchtime came and went, the venue started bustling. There was a time early afternoon when there was an influx of people. Some of the staff switched over. Drake and Alicia had been told to work an eight-hour shift, but they noticed nobody actually kept track of the timings. At least, no one obvious. Maybe there was an opportunity to hang around a bit longer. As the hours passed, Drake found himself once more near Quigley.

A new question had come to mind. 'Does the tsar have his own security detail?'

'Why do you ask?'

'It might be good to get on it.'

Quigley grunted. 'Yeah, and they're all bastards. Would shoot you just as look at you. Assholes, the lot of them. I wouldn't want to work with that lot.'

Drake nodded his thanks, happy they'd learned something else about the tsar. He kept his eyes on the curtains, hoping they'd twitch open, but nothing happened.

They stayed past their allotted hour. Nobody approached them. Five became six and then half past. The place was filling. Drake saw men dressed in suits who looked like gangsters, women wearing long sparkling dresses, taking people aside and doing business. He saw the dancers, the hangers-on, the players and their aides. People were here to have a good time, to get drunk, to party and dance and to do a little business. He fancied most of them would give their right arm to chomp at the tsar's ear.

Of him, there was still no sign.

They stuck to their jobs, bored out of their minds, but knowing they were in the right place. All they needed was opportunity.

Drake, searching the bar area as the place grew busier, suddenly locked eyes on one of the women. His heart leapt.

Mai!

To her right, he saw both Kenzie and Hayden. The women were clad in form hugging dresses, their make-up subtle, their hair hanging down. They appeared to be performing a hostess role, mingling and chatting and keeping the clients happy. As the place filled, there were always plenty of people to butter up.

Drake tapped Alicia and nodded in their direction. Alicia said, 'Nice,' and looked away. Together, they wandered in their general direction and waited until Mai had seen them and gave them a subtle nod. That was not quite enough, though. Mai wandered closer, and Drake leaned over to whisper in her ear.

'We've seen Mano and Dahl. Have you seen Cam and Shaw?'

Mai licked her lips and then put a hand on Drake's arm, laughing. 'Good to hear the first part. No sign of Cam and Shaw.'

Drake continued past as if nothing had happened. He searched the room for the thousandth time and worried about Cam and Shaw. Where the hell were they? Could they already have filtered through to the tsar's inner circle?

Well done, if they had. If not... Drake was worried.

CHAPTER THIRTY ONE

The Dark Tsar pushed hard on his cross trainer, sweat dripping from his forehead all over the equipment. His legs ached, the muscles of his back were taut. He liked to stay fit, and devoted a considerable amount of time each day to doing so. The exercise also helped him think, solidifying things in his mind.

He was alone, save for a couple of guards. There were also guards stationed outside the door. As he worked and sweated, his mind flicked over the latest reports that might affect his empire. Reports from Javier, from other trusted sources, from the covert CCTV cameras he used throughout the castle. Inside knowledge was extremely important.

The tsar plotted and planned and watched what went on in his world. He finished on the cross trainer, climbed off, and went for a quick shower. Next, he dressed in an expensive suit and entered a quiet room. This area was completely enclosed, had soundproofing tiles on the walls, a thick carpet, and a chair and a table. It also had a large TV on one wall. The tsar sat back with a bottle of vodka and a cut-glass tumbler, knocking one back. He sighed. What came next?

His thoughts turned first to the jobs at hand.

There was a new arms deal on the way. A new client he really wanted to trust. Something that was difficult after the last attempt failed so badly. He'd lost four men that day, but they had come through, eliminating the bad guys in such a way that sent a powerful message. *Do not fuck with the tsar.*

Of course, all of this paled next to the main event. There would be a new hospital attack in three days. There were six hospitals left to bomb, three weeks left to go. He was enjoying his newfound popularity and the fact that law enforcement just couldn't find him. He'd been consummately brilliant at covering his tracks, at leaving false leads, and he congratulated himself for it. The hospital attacks were a fantastic idea.

The tsar poured himself another drink. He turned his thoughts to new developments. Two new thieves had come along – named Cam and Shaw – who were showing potential. They had very good reps, and were being whisked here right now. At speed. The purpose being that he had a special job for them.

The tsar narrowed his eyes. For a while now, he'd been looking at stealing a pile of nuclear detonators. The detonators were in Croatia, stored in some top secret, well-guarded warehouse, and he'd lacked the expertise to grab them. Now, though, the appearance of the new thieves might just change all that. He could give them an important mission almost immediately. If he could procure the detonators... he smiled in the dark room, his eyes black as an abyss. That would open up endless possibilities.

Also, he'd taken on new procurers, new guards and new entertainers. The tsar was always made aware when this happened... it all added to his vulnerabilities. But the new people had been vetted, they came highly recommended and Javier had met at least two of them at random. It was the best he could do to continue to hide his activities.

And the entertainers might be interesting.

The tsar loved new women. The opposite sex was a huge part of his life and one reason he loved being the main man. If he could, he would have a new woman every night, but here, under the circumstances, it just wasn't viable. But the thought of three new entertainers filled him with expectation.

The tsar thought about his inner circle, the men and women who guarded his back, who really looked after him. There was Javier, of course, his second-in-command, but there was also the inner circle of guards, the lesser beings who fetched and carried for him. They were trusted, tried, experienced. He actually depended on them. In truth, a man in his position shouldn't depend on anyone. But it was the reality of his situation. He couldn't do all this alone.

The only way someone could get close to him was through an invitation.

And that didn't happen often. He made an exception for the women, of course – most of them. He was actually a highly capable, trained martial artist and this too he practiced every day. He was happy that he could take care of himself if a dangerous situation ever arose. His next challenge was to train in firearms. Of course, you could never be entirely certain that one of the beauties he enticed to his bedroom wasn't an undercover, trained assassin, but those were risks he was willing to take for incredible company.

The tsar found a remote and clicked it at the TV. The screen flashed into life. On it, there were various views of the castle – rooms and corridors and open spaces, even the outside perimeter if he wanted it. He focused now on the main venue where he'd be headed soon, picked out the familiar faces among the crowd and the not so familiar.

It looked busy tonight. That was good. He liked a pliable crowd, fresh people. Of course, few of them knew his true identity – they just assumed this was another rich, bored man's party chateau.

The tsar started as his phone began to ring. He fished it out of his pocket, checked the screen. *Javier.*

It was unusual for his second-in-command to call him on the phone. The man usually waited to see him in person.

'What's wrong?' The tsar asked, knowing this couldn't be good.

'We may have a problem. An internal problem.'

'Go on.'

'The new arrivals.'

The tsar frowned. 'Which ones?'

'They go by the names Cam and Shaw.'

The tsar experienced a sinking feeling. 'The special thieves?'

'Yes, the special thieves.'

'I had high hopes for them. Explain this to me.'

'They're snoopers. Right from the start. Asking questions, mostly about you and our location. Raised a red flag, so I checked with the source. He said they were recommended to him by Slow Jack. Remember him?'

The tsar had a vague recollection of a dirty, smelly, badly dressed contact who he was occasionally forced to do business with. 'Unfortunately, yes.'

'I checked with Slow Jack. Said he'd never heard of them. Not as thieves, not as human beings. Which means all their recommendations were fabricated.'

The tsar let out a long breath. 'So they're what? Spies?'

'I think they're here for you.'

It was a reasonable assumption. The tsar cursed under his breath. He didn't need this kind of hassle right now. 'How about the other recent newcomers?'

'They check out perfectly from a different source. They're all okay.'

'Good. Well, at least that's one bonus. The question is – what are we going to do about Cam and Shaw?'

'A bullet to the head would be a good idea.'

'Maybe, but I don't like the timing of this. Someone has infiltrated my organisation at the very moment I have come more into the limelight, at the time of the hospital bombings. We can't be sure this isn't a wider conspiracy.'

'What are you suggesting?'

'That you torture the information out of them, Javier. That you wring out everything they know, piece by piece, if you have to.'

Javier was silent for a while. The tsar knew he wasn't a 'hands-on' kind of guy when it came to torture. He would pass it on to someone else and was probably trying to decide just how to do that.

'You think they have accomplices?' Javier finally asked.

'I think it's a possibility, and we need to know. I'd suggest you get yourself a plan together and get on with it.'

'Of course. Do you not think we might use them first?'

The tsar considered it. If Cam and Shaw were the consummate thieves they were purported to be, maybe he *could* use them. He really needed those detonators. But then – if they were spies or assassins, did he really want them lingering inside his organisation?

'The next bombing is in just a few days,' he said. 'Let's see what we can get out of them before then.'

Javier agreed and signed off. The tsar replaced his phone, angry at being infiltrated, feeling let down by his trusted contacts. Someone would pay for this in the long run, maybe several someones. He flicked the CCTV back on and consoled himself by checking several camera views of the entertainment venue. He would soon be there, the chief attraction. Tonight would be a good night.

And soon, in three days, he would take further vengeance on the world.

CHAPTER THIRTY TWO

Drake and Alicia pulled a later shift that day. They arrived in the main room late afternoon and started their usual rounds. They were fully aware of the approaching deadline for the hospital bombing and were full of anxiety. Somehow, they had to get close to the tsar. And they had to do it tonight.

There was something nice waiting for them in the room, though. It seemed Kinimaka and Dahl had been invited to party with the others. They were seated in a far corner, looking decidedly uncomfortable, but trying to blend in as best they could. Drake and Alicia made sure they passed close and then stopped behind their friend's seats.

'How's it going?' Drake asked.

'No chance to get close yet,' Dahl said. 'Even here, the guy's a ghost.'

'How about you?' Kinimaka asked.

'Yesterday was a bust,' Alicia said. 'Hoping for better things tonight.'

'Any news from the others?' Dahl asked.

Drake looked up at that moment, saw Hayden coming towards him. Behind her were Mai and Kenzie, passing among the guests. It was right then that, over in another far corner, he saw Cam and Shaw. For a brief moment, the entire team was aware of each other.

The moment passed necessarily quickly. Drake felt both contentment and anxiety that they were all there, all in the belly of the beast.

Hayden came up to them, pretending to chat to Dahl and Kinimaka. 'How's it going?'

They went through the same questions and answers as they had a few moments ago. Nobody had managed to get close to the tsar yet.

'Even in his own home, he's a bloody ghost,' Drake reiterated.

Mai came up to them then, also pretending to engage in conversation with them. Kenzie soon joined them. They didn't stay together for long, didn't want to create any kind of spectacle or draw attention, but they managed a brief discussion.

'Tonight, we try,' Mai said. 'We take this bastard down.'

'We got this far,' Dahl said. 'Almost there.'

'Be ready for anything,' Drake said. 'We've heard he has a pretty tough detail around him.'

'Guards?' Mai asked.

'Yeah. A proper inner circle.'

The Japanese woman grunted. They moved apart then, the three women moving on, chatting to other guests. Drake and Alicia drifted away from Dahl and Kinimaka and continued their patrol of the room. They recognised the same faces as last night, including Quigley, with a few exceptions. One guy wearing a tux and black jacket appeared not to have moved in twenty-four hours, surrounded by a bevy of blondes both male and female. He drank spirits out of a wine glass and had placed a stiletto knife on the table in front of him, as if daring the guards to complain. Nobody approached him, so Drake and Alicia stayed away.

Time passed. Drake felt his anxiety levels increase as still they faced limbo. They passed close to Cam and Shaw but didn't stop to speak, thinking yet again that they should be seen to remain aloof from most of the guests.

Drake was despairing. Yes, they'd only been on the inside for a day or so, but there was still no sign of...

He stopped in his tracks. The plush black curtains that covered the tsar's special room were twitching. He saw a hand reaching through, grabbing one half. Next, the curtains were drawn back. Drake tried not to let his staring appear too obvious. The room revealed was wide and deep. Reflections on the glass made it hard to make out much detail, but he saw several men in suits and lots of leather chairs. The room had its own bar, behind which a male and a female were serving.

'I'm counting twelve,' Alicia said. 'And the place isn't even crowded.'

Drake nodded. Slowly, they made towards the room, trying to see deeper inside. Of course, they didn't know what the tsar looked like, but thought he'd make a pretty obvious figure once he made an appearance. Drake turned to Alicia.

'We know that's his room,' he said. 'Shall we try?'

CHAPTER THIRTY THREE

Drake and Alicia started for the room. Drake saw that Kinimaka and Dahl had also risen to their feet, but now sat down and he wondered if they'd had the same plan. They skirted the perimeter until they stood outside the door to the tsar's room.

Drake looked inside, getting his first proper view. The room was vast and plushly decorated. Besides the bar, he saw a plethora of tables and sofas and bean bag nests. The men in suits were standing at ease, looking around, slightly bored. There were several TVs on the walls and a large free-standing globe at the centre of the room. The globe was half open, bottles of alcohol glistening. The lighting was muted. As Drake watched, the bar staff handed out several drinks and there was a touch of laughter. Everyone inside seemed at ease.

Right then, one of the men saw Drake staring through the glass. He patted his friend on the shoulder. Both men appeared to sigh and then came walking over and opened the door.

Drake was ready for them. 'Hey,' he said, refraining from his usual Yorkshire greeting.

'What do you want?' the tallest of the two men asked in a bored voice.

'We're looking for the tsar,' Drake said. 'Any chance of an audience?'

All the time, he was checking the men for weapons. So far, he'd clocked a handgun and a knife on each man. There was no sign of any serious assault rifles.

'The tsar isn't here yet. Are you new or something?'

Drake said that they were.

'I'll give you a piece of advice. The tsar doesn't take kindly to cold callers, especially when he's in his favourite room. If you want to stay on his good side, I'd leave him the fuck alone.'

'Not even me?' Alicia asked. Drake remembered the tsar had a soft spot for women.

'Well, you, he'd definitely see, but not in the capacity you're expecting,' the man grinned. 'If you know what I mean.'

'Want some of that, do ya?' the other man asked.

Drake stepped in, not wanting to go that far yet. 'How would someone get an audience with him?'

'Go through your immediate superior. Run it up the chain of command. It's pretty obvious when you think about it.'

The tall man closed the door, expecting them to walk away. Drake and Alicia did just that, not wanting to blow their cover. They started on the perimeter again, giving Kinimaka and Hayden a shake of their heads.

They'd failed.

Kinimaka and Dahl rose to their feet.

Dahl started across the room and glanced sideways at the Hawaiian. 'Let me do the talking.'

'You think that's wise? If he insults you, you'll just throw him through a window.'

'I'll try to refrain.'

'Please do. We're in a good position where we are.'

Dahl made his way to the newly revealed room and stared inside. Soon, the same two men who had confronted Drake and Alicia opened the door.

'Yes?' the tall one was clearly pissed off.

'We're the tsar's new procurers,' Dahl said. 'We've been here a few days and haven't heard a thing. Just wondering if we could come in, you know, get a feel for the inner circle. Maybe get issued a job?'

'A job? That would come down from your immediate superior. Do you know who that is?'

Dahl nodded as Kinimaka fought to remain silent. 'Yeah.'

'Then talk to him,' the tall man started to close the door in the Swede's face.

Kinimaka put his foot in the gap. 'One second,' he said. 'We didn't come all the way here to sit around and get drunk. We came to work.'

There was a moment's surprised silence. The tall man blinked. 'Look,' he said, trying to keep the peace. 'The tsar passes jobs down as and when they come up. He can't just materialise one out of thin air. Chill out. You're still getting paid.'

Dahl looked over the man's shoulder. 'Any chance of talking to him about that?'

'He's not here yet,' a note of exasperation entered the man's voice. 'Give me a break.'

Now he managed to get the door shut as Kinimaka backed down. They simply couldn't push it any further. Together, they turned away, Dahl giving his watching friends a shake of his head and a shrug. They'd tried their best for now.

'A lot of security in there,' Dahl whispered to Kinimaka. 'And if they're all special forces, it's gonna be hard.'

'We've done hard before,' Kinimaka said, nodding as they passed Hayden near the centre of the room.

'Now,' she said. 'It's our turn.'

Hayden, Kenzie and Mai all wore matching outfits – modest enough flowing dresses that went down to their knees. The dresses were black and fairly tight. But they weren't here to be stared at – they were here to butter up the clients, to make their nights better, to make them spend more money and perhaps gamble a little at the three tables set up in a far corner. Now, the three of them walked right up to the window of the tsar's room.

Hayden smiled at the tall man, who once again came straight to the door. He popped his head out. 'Can I help you all?'

'What do you have to do to get in there?' Mai asked with a tilt of her head.

The tall man bit his bottom lip as if holding back all sorts of replies. His eyes betrayed his thoughts as he looked the three of them over. 'You have to be invited,' he said eventually. 'By the boss.'

Hayden noticed the usage of the word boss instead of tsar. Of course, not everyone who worked for the tsar knew his real identity. This man would assume the entertainment staff would fall into that category.

'And how do you get an invitation?' Kenzie asked.

'Look, he's not here yet. I can't let you in. How about you come back later?'

Just then, a far door opened, and a man walked through. He was clad in a black suit and wore black shoes. He wore no jewellery. His face was striking, and he looked fit and healthy, as if he worked out every day before jumping under a sunbed. The man went straight to the bar and spoke to one of the servers. Instantly, they handed him a drink, as if the beverage had been prepared and was waiting for him.

'Is that the boss?' Mai asked.

The tall man looked back. 'Oh, yeah. That's him.'

It was their first proper look at the tsar.

Hayden hoped Drake and the others were watching too, and threw a quick glance over her shoulder to check. They were. Everyone now had a fair idea of what the tsar looked like. At least, tonight, that was something they'd succeeded at.

'How about now?' Mai asked. 'Any chance we can talk to him?'

The tall man shook his head. 'No. It just came through on the earpiece,' he tapped his left ear. 'Problems. The boss is in a foul mood. Doesn't want to speak to anyone.'

Hayden cursed their luck. They couldn't push it any further. With a gracious nod, they backed away and resumed their duties. It just wasn't their night. Hayden looked over to Cam and Shaw and shrugged as if to say 'give it a shot.'

Both Cam and Shaw rose to their feet. They had possibly the best reason to approach the tsar. They were regarded as the very best of thieves. In reality, he should appreciate their interest and might even decide to give them an audience. Maybe they could help assuage his mood.

Hayden glad-handed a few guests, keeping an eye on Cam and Shaw as they slowly strolled around the room. They were about thirty feet from the door when there came a *bing bong* over the tannoy system and a loud voice spoke over the music. Hayden likened it to a train station – except this was an announcement they could actually hear – but it was certainly effective and caught everyone's attention.

'This is a shout out for Cam and Shaw. Please report to your station so that you can receive instructions. Repeat, Cam and Shaw. There is a new job for you.'

Hayden saw the couple freeze in their tracks. They looked shocked, but met Hayden's eyes and gave a brief nod. She smiled back weakly. She hadn't even known about the tannoy, but she guessed it was an effective tool.

Cam and Shaw turned and walked out of the room together.

Hayden watched them go.

CHAPTER THIRTY FOUR

Cam walked easily with Shaw at his side, his face a tranquil mask. Inside, he was feeling a raft of emotions, everything from fear to anxiety to excitement and tension. He fought hard to keep his face smooth, his eyes steady.

They were going to be the first to get close to the tsar. At least, he hoped so. Hoped a subordinate wouldn't hand them their first assignment.

They found their immediate superior and presented themselves to him. He raised an eyebrow, which again made Cam frown, and then gave a nod.

'Follow me,' he said.

They entered one of the far offices, walked through and then exited by a door in the back. They traversed a wide corridor, turned right at a branch, and then followed another long passageway, moving further and further away from the entertainment venue. At the end of the passage, Cam saw a door.

Two men were standing outside, both armed. When they saw Cam and Shaw approaching, they raised their guns. Cam felt the tension running a little higher. 'Whoa,' Shaw said. 'What's with the aggression?'

The men said nothing, just knocked on the door and then moved aside. Almost immediately, the door was opened, revealing a large room lit by stark spotlights. Cam saw a plastic table, chairs, and several long plastic benches. He and Shaw entered the room.

Something heavy smacked him over the back of the head. Cam staggered forward, grabbing for the table to steady himself. Out of the corner of his eye, he saw Shaw also fall forward as someone clouted her on the back of the head.

Cam swung around in a boxer's stance, fists clenched. A large man stood facing him, a grim expression on his face. Cam didn't waste time talking. He struck out with his fists, two low blows and an uppercut, making the man stagger badly. Cam gripped his wrist, but the man held on to his gun.

Shaw fell to her knees, then kicked out backwards, catching her opponent mid-thigh. The man staggered and yelled out as Shaw swivelled and came at him from her position on the floor. Her legs kicked out, catching him on the ankles and knees. He collapsed, landing flat on his face, the gun trapped underneath him.

From within the room, more figures came running. Cam caught a quick glimpse, saw seven or eight armed men. What the hell was going on? He rose swiftly, approached the first, hit him hard in the fae. The man went down, blood flowing from a broken nose, hitting the floor hard.

His gun clattered away.

Cam dived for it. Before he could reach it, a man jumped in and smacked him across the forehead with the butt of his weapon. Cam saw stars, wavered. He held on, still punching, trying to stay strong. He stepped in close and punched the man in the gut, saw many weapons now covering him. One man said, 'Stand down.'

Shaw was still on the floor, looking up at several barrels pointed down at her. She raised her hands. 'What are you doing?' She asked.

As Cam's victims groaned and tried to pick themselves up off the floor, he was led to one of the plastic chairs and thrown roughly into it. Then, his hands were cuffed behind his back. To his right, Shaw was treated similarly. He caught her eyes, conveyed a look of concern. All around them, men with guns stared down in silence.

'We're just here for our assignment,' Cam said evenly. 'I think there's been a mistake.'

The absence of words hung heavy in the air. Cam coughed, looked around. The room, though large, was just a square. The benches running along both sides were full of small boxes and pouches. He saw wrecking bars and drills and a set of knives. There was even a baseball bat at one end. A man saw him eyeing up the implements and gave him a little sneer.

Eventually, a far door opened. A balding man stepped through, seemingly in a hurry. He cast his eyes over the captives.

'You'll be wondering why you're here,' he said. 'I'm Javier, the tsar's second-in-command. You're Cam and Shaw, the *special* thieves. Am I right?'

Cam saw no reason not to keep up the pretence. 'Is this some kind of test? If so, it's in pretty poor taste.'

'No test,' Javier said. 'I want you to meet someone.'

The Dark Tsar

And he stepped aside. Another man walked through the door, an impeccably dressed man. Cam recognised him instantly as the Dark Tsar. Javier stepped aside as the man addressed them.

'You are causing me immense trouble. I have need of a capable set of thieves right now. And here you are, in my lap. But I can't use you. Do you know why?'

Cam tried to look bewildered. 'We are here. I have no idea.'

'Because you're a pair of dirty, filthy snakes,' the tsar growled. 'Yes, you've been betrayed. You're spies. Spies in my ranks. And I want to know everything that you know.'

Despite the situation, Cam felt a touch of irony spike through him. Here they were, exactly where they wanted to be – next to the Dark Tsar – and there was nothing they could do about it. The whole point of the mission was to get within striking distance of this man...

Cam bit his lip in frustration.

'My contacts are greater than yours, it seems,' the tsar went on. 'More loyal. They ratted you out, my friends.' The tsar seemed to love the idea, love the feeling of power it gave him, the feeling of betrayal it must give Cam and Shaw. He came close to them. *Within killing distance,* Cam thought. He shook his head, again feeling frustration.

The tsar mistook his expression for disappointment. 'I'd feel the same,' he said. 'If it happened to me.'

Cam didn't want to give up yet. The mission was too important. 'Whatever you've been told, it's a lie.

You've been betrayed. We're the real deal and we can prove it to you. Just untie us. Let us loose on this mission.' He readied himself, hands clenched, ready to leap on the tsar.

'Nice try. So tell me Cam and Shaw, if that's your real names. Why are you really here? What's your objective?'

'And who do you work for?' Javier added.

Cam opened his mouth but didn't speak. Beside him, Shaw tried again. 'We *are* thieves,' she said. 'Damn good ones. And we want to work for you. What can it hurt to let us try?'

The tsar's lips tightened into a white line. 'You've infiltrated my organisation. The first to do so. But...' he shrugged. 'Have you really? You were led here into my trap. I'm not sure that's a successful mission on your part. But you *are* here. And you have an aim. What is it?'

To stop and kill you, you mad bastard, Cam thought, but said nothing. Instead, his eyes flicked around the room. 'All I can say is, you're barking up the wrong tree.'

The tsar looked confused. 'What?'

Cam wondered if Drake's use of English was rubbing off on him. 'You're mistaken,' he said. 'You've got it all wrong.'

The tsar gave him a speculative stare. Maybe now he was questioning his own contacts. 'There's a chance you're right,' he said. 'Maybe I am being played. But I like to think the people I deal with fear me too much to try that. They fear my wrath. And I am good at vengeance.'

Cam knew it was a reference to the hospital

bombings and said nothing. There was no right answer.

'Anyway, it has been nice,' the tsar straightened. 'But now I will hand you over to the capable hands of this man, Melchior. We call him the Maestro of Pain.' With a small smile, the tsar indicated a rail thin man to his left. Cam thought the man resembled a walking cadaver; his cheeks were hollowed out, and he had dark eyes and thin, bony wrists. His fingers were long and delicate, though, giving him the appearance of an alien. Cam couldn't stop a shiver of fear crawling through him.

'What the hell?' Shaw said.

'I think I'll stay and watch,' the tsar said with a grin.

Behind him, Javier left the room. The man named Melchior went over to one of the benches and started picking through the implements. He raised a screwdriver speculatively, glanced at Cam, then gave a skeletal smile and put it back. Next, he pulled a steak knife from the rack, ram his finger along the edge, and then put it back.

'This is always a great game,' the tsar said with an evil grin. 'Does he go subtle, or does he go big?'

Melchior picked up the crowbar and raised it to eye level. He then gave Cam a satisfied smirk. The tsar coughed. 'Big,' he said. 'This will be bad for you. I'm going to give you one last chance to come clean. Answer my questions now.'

Cam struggled in his bonds as Melchior approached. He really didn't know how he was feeling – it was all a rush of emotion. All he knew was that he'd never been in this position before, and he was really hoping that Drake and the others would crash in and save the day.

Melchior stopped by Cam's right side. He signalled the gun-toting men who stood around. Quickly, they uncuffed Cam and then tied his hands to the arms of the chair with plastic cuffs. He didn't understand at first. When he was untied, he considered fighting back, but there were two men with their guns levelled at his head and another one pointing a weapon at his knees. There were also the men covering Shaw. Cam let the opportunity slide, lasting in character for as long as he could.

Now Melchior tapped the crowbar against his wrist, where it lay atop the arm of the chair. He gave Cam his skeletal grin, a sight that sent another shiver through the boxer. 'It is now or never,' Melchior said in a high, lilting voice.

Cam stared the tsar defiantly in the eyes. 'You are making a mistake,' he said. 'Let us help you.'

Melchior glanced at the tsar. The boss gave a nod. Melchior raised the crowbar and brought it down with immense force, smashing it onto Cam's wrist. Cam saw it coming, braced, and then felt an intense flash of agony in his right wrist. The bone broke – he heard the crack. He couldn't stop the scream from escaping.

Melchior smiled and stepped back. The tsar stepped in, grabbed Cam by the throat, and lifted his chin. 'Tell me everything,' he said.

Cam seethed, feeling pain course through his body. His wrist shrieked at him. He bucked back and forth in the chair, shaking his head.

'Break her wrist next,' the tsar said. 'We'll do them alternately.'

Cam screamed *'No!'* as Melchior moved over to Shaw and oversaw the tying of her arms to the chair. Next, he raised his crowbar as he grinned into Shaw's eyes. 'Ready?' he asked.

She said nothing. The crowbar came down, and she cried out in agony. Cam heard her wrist break. Melchior walked back over to him.

'Elbow,' he said.

Cam stared despairingly at the tsar. All he got back was an open expression, as if the man was telling him to come clean. Cam wouldn't do it. He would take the pain, and so would Shaw.

The crowbar came down again.

CHAPTER THIRTY FIVE

Time passed slowly for Drake and the others. They did their jobs, walked their perimeters and entertained their guests. Acted as part of the festivities, and waited for something to happen. After Cam and Shaw were called to their assignment, Drake noticed the tsar disappeared. He hoped this meant he was briefing Cam and Shaw. It would give them a chance to get close to him. He and Alicia both waited expectantly, on edge, but the minutes passed and then an hour and nothing happened. They did their jobs, unsure. Maybe Cam and Shaw had been forced to actually undertake a mission. That would be unfortunate because, with time against them, there were only two days to the next hospital bombing. The night passed in slow anguish.

Their shift ended without incident. The tsar returned. Drake and Alicia watched him, getting a feel for his proclivities, his likes and dislikes, the way he ignored male attention and invited female, the appetites he displayed for champagne and forties music and any woman he could lay his eyes on. It seemed you had to be invited to his inner room and, tonight, he seemed a little distracted, barely glancing out into the main room.

Which put Mai, Hayden and Kenzie at a

disadvantage. They had been hoping to get noticed. Tonight, though, the tsar appeared to have other things on his mind.

Drake and Alicia eventually made it back to their room. They felt deflated, unsure. Drake sat on the edge of his bed, looking at Alicia.

'I can only think Cam and Shaw didn't get a chance to strike and have been sent on a mission,' he said. 'That's the only thing that makes sense.'

'Yeah. He definitely disappeared for a while, but that doesn't mean he went off to see them. Who knows? Maybe they got their instructions from Javier or some other goon.'

Drake bit his lip. 'Two days to go,' he said. 'We're gonna have to pull off something special.'

'We could all assault the room together,' Alicia said. 'Put Dahl in front 'cos he's bulletproof.'

'Ordinarily I'd say yes,' Drake said. 'But let's not go that far just yet.'

They got into bed, tried to sleep. The night passed slowly and fitfully. The next day, they hit the mess hall and started asking questions.

Drake located a bored-looking man who appeared to be a seasoned veteran of the castle. He was grizzled and grey and regarded everyone with an air of resignation.

'Have you been around a while?' he asked.

The man just stared at him.

'I'm looking for some advice.'

'Shoot.'

'All right then. Well, I want to get into the inner circle. I think it'd be a better job with better pay. What I do – it's boring. I'm not cut out for wandering the edges of a glorified nightclub. Any ideas how I can get into the inner circle?'

The grizzled man laughed. 'You and everyone else,' he said. 'I've resigned myself to staying where I am. The pay's not so bad. It can take months, if not years, to gain the tsar's inner circle. He isn't exactly trusting.'

Drake didn't have to feign disappointment. 'Months? Years?'

'Afraid so. I've been here for nine months and never seen anyone promoted.'

Drake thanked him and walked away. At the table, he related what he'd been told to Alicia. They ate in silence, whiling away the time. Half way through their meal they saw Dahl and Kinimaka enter and managed to get close.

'Seen anything of Cam and Shaw?' Dahl asked.

Drake shook his head. 'Can only assume they've been sent out on a mission.'

'Or caught,' Dahl said ominously.

'Why do you say that?'

'They didn't use Crouch. They used a different contact. Seemed like a good idea at the time.'

'It was a good idea,' Drake said. 'But if they have gone out on a mission, God knows when we'll see them again.'

It felt odd, as if the team was tearing itself apart. Drake didn't like it, didn't like not knowing what was happening.

'Seen any chances to get close to the tsar?' he asked.

Kinimaka shook his head. 'Still waiting for our assignment.'

'It has only been a couple of days, in truth,' Alicia said. 'We're expecting too many things to happen too quickly.'

On their way out, they bumped into Mai, Hayden and Kenzie, but didn't get a chance to talk. It was good to see the rest of the team, though, to know everyone was still firmly in the game. The rest of the morning passed in anxious silence, feeling like a waste to Drake. They went for a walk, trawled the castle halls, but saw no chance of getting closer to the tsar. They didn't even know here he spent the days and asking would only draw attention to them. If anything, they were hoping for a chance encounter.

Nothing happened.

It drew close to their next shift. They tooled up again, made their way to the venue. Again, there were the usual suspects, and they started their rounds.

Later, the tsar appeared once more. Tonight, he looked even more agitated and barely glanced out the window. Drake saw his team again doing their respective jobs – Kinimaka and Dahl lounging around in stasis, Hayden and the other two women glad-handing the guests and fending off advances.

Time weighed heavily on them. The night passed in a relative agony, every second just leeching away. The tsar's inner layer of security watched him well, their eyes everywhere. They were good, Drake noted, never letting their attention drift for a second. He made several passes of the room, drifting towards the glass to test them, and was tracked every time he got close. He wondered if he should just shoot the tsar through the glass.

Of course, it would be bulletproof, and then his chance would be gone. Along with his life.

The night passed. They followed their routine. Now there was only one day left before the next deadline. Drake and Alicia fretted over it, not knowing what to do. All they needed was the glimmer of a chance.

It didn't arrive. The next day dawned, and they followed the same rigmarole. They got next to the glass, spoke through the door, but were not invited inside. The tsar didn't even look at them. Kinimaka and Dahl tried again, and they were admitted, but only for a few seconds. Guns covered them the whole time and soon they emerged, shaking their heads. Mai and the others also tried their luck, but didn't even get past the door. The tsar didn't see them, so engrossed was he in something else. And in fact, when he didn't see the women, his guards looked relieved as if they'd escaped a pain-in-the-arse few hours watching their boss flirt. Again, he disappeared for a while, returning close to the end of Drake's shift.

And then they were done. Another night gone. They woke on the day of the next bombing and were no further forward. They followed the same routine, despairing. The tsar had six more bombings planned in total.

And there was no way to stop this one.

CHAPTER THIRTY SIX

It was early evening. Drake would never forget it. The whole day had started as any other – showering, the mess hall, the boredom, the shift – trying to figure out a way to get close to the tsar, wondering how Cam and Shaw were faring, trying to communicate with each other and come up with something new, but today – this day – there was something more.

A dark and terrible foreboding.

It could happen anytime, and they might not even know, but the bar area had a TV, and they made sure at least one of them was in its vicinity the entire day.

But nothing happened.

They communicated with a shake of their heads. They watched the curtained room, tried to assess the tension between guards to see if there was anything different. But there was nothing. Could the tsar have called the bombing off?

But, in his heart, Drake knew that would never happen. The day was far from done. He started his shift with Alicia and kept his eyes on the patrons, stepping in where necessary. He did this himself, keeping Alicia well away. She wasn't exactly diplomatic.

Around the usual time, the curtains twitched and then opened, revealing the tsar's room and everyone inside. Tonight, Drake saw, there was an unusual amount of suited guards hovering around the tsar, all with their guns in evidence. The very first thing the tsar did was turn on a large screen TV.

Drake met Dahl's eyes and spread his arms. *What can we do?*

The Swede looked equally downcast. He gave Drake a small shake of his head. Drake looked at Hayden, who had just come in from the bar.

'Any information?'

She shook her head. 'Nothing. It's just another dull day.'

'He just made an appearance and switched on the TV. Looks like he's up to something in there.'

Hayden gazed into the room. 'I don't like the look of that.'

Drake turned. The entire ensemble was getting settled, drinks in hand, feet up, leaning back in their chairs. The tsar was at the centre of it all, laughing and gesturing and grabbing the attention. He looked to be having a great time.

'What are they doing?' Drake asked.

'Shame we can't hear them,' Hayden was referring to the soundproofed glass.

Drake knew their situation was becoming desperate. They were at the end of everything here. But what could they do? Surrounded by guards, facing an implacable enemy who was surrounded by even better guards. And half the people in here didn't even know how deadly their benefactor was.

As Drake watched, the activity in the room died down. The men watched the TV with rapt attention. Some of them kept glancing at their watches, drinking, eating. Drake saw the channel was a news station.

He knew exactly what they were doing. Didn't want to – he wanted to refute it, to force it all away – but the signs were obvious. He turned to Hayden.

'I can't believe this.'

'It's disgusting.'

He checked his watch. It was three minutes to eight. The men inside the room were leaning forward, their eyes fixed on the TV screen. They drank and drank, their drinks being topped up by a wandering barman. The tsar looked to be the only one truly at ease, sitting with one leg crossed over the other, an arm draped across his chair, drink in the other hand. Drake could only see the back of his head, but assumed there was a self-satisfied smile on that face.

Two minutes to eight.

He checked his gun, took in the positions of the guards, checked the positioning of his team. Right then, Hayden put a hand on his arm.

'Don't. You'll die.'

'We have to do *something*.'

'We are doing something. We're right here in the dragon's lair. Just waiting for a chance. Cam and Shaw might even meet with him later, for all we know. You can't just throw that away now.'

Drake felt torn. Hayden was right. They had successfully infiltrated an inaccessible organisation, gone in right under their enemy's noses. They were right here, in the best place, just waiting for their chance. But it wasn't happening soon enough. Drake hated the waiting. It wasn't him. Usually he was jumping headlong into the next dollop of action, and then the next, and that was fine. But this... he couldn't stand the delaying.

Hayden squeezed his arm. 'Wait,' she said. 'It's the right thing to do.'

Drake's watch clicked past eight o'clock. The men in the room were all fully focused on the TV. The guards too. Even the tsar had leaned forward. Nobody drank. Nobody spoke. They all seemed to be waiting for something.

Drake took a deep breath and removed his hand from his gun. It was one of the hardest things he'd ever done – to do nothing – and his fingers shook slightly.

From the room there came a sudden loud cheer, heavily muted through the soundproofed glass. In fact, Drake might have imagined the noise. He saw the activity.

The men surged to their feet, spilling their drinks and punching the air. They were ecstatic, turning to each other and clapping backs and shoulders. Some of them jumped. All were watching the TV.

Drake could barely see through their shoulders, but managed to make out a screen with a 'Breaking News' ticker running along the bottom. The picture showed a smoking building.

Some men were whooping, holding each other, others just yelling in pleasure. Drake had never seen a more disgusting, appalling display. Amongst it all, he could now see the tsar smiling modestly and receiving congratulations.

As he watched, Drake saw more snippets of the screen. One shot showed a picture taken from a drone of a smoking building, a quarter of one side blown away. Another closer shot showed a crumbling façade, worsening as they watched. It showed fleeing men and women, hospital patients and workers.

And through it all, the men cheered at what they had wrought.

Without knowing it, Drake realised his fingers had gripped the barrel of his gun. His knuckles were white, his teeth clenched together. As this side, Hayden had done the same and, despite her earlier warnings, had already taken a step towards the tsar's room.

Kinimaka appeared before them, a great looming shape.

'Stand down,' he said.

'Look at them,' Drake said. 'They don't deserve to live.'

'Agreed, but you do, and now is not the time.'

Dahl was to Drake's left. 'He's right. You know me. But this is no time to go and get yourselves killed.' The Swede looked like he wanted to take a bite from someone, but he held out a hand of restraint.

Alicia was to Drake's right. She met his gaze and gave him a nod. 'Not now,' she said.

'Then fucking when?' he blurted. 'We've been arsing around here long enough.'

'When the opportunity presents itself,' Kinimaka said.

'It's not gonna present itself,' Drake said, aware they were making a scene but not caring. 'The bastard's too well guarded.'

'He doesn't make any mistakes,' Hayden said.

Dahl looked once more at the room where the

men and the tsar were partying. 'He will,' he said. 'And we'll be there to take him out.'

'We could do it right now,' Drake said quietly. 'We have enough people.'

Dahl assessed the room, took in the positions of the guards, counted them. 'We do, but how will we get into that room?'

Drake didn't know and hung his head. 'We've failed,' he said.

A deep silence hung around him, the others all thinking the same thing. Drake couldn't look at the room anymore, couldn't bear to see the celebrations. The tsar looked more relaxed than Drake had ever seen him, and now he wondered if the man had been worrying heavily about the bombing over the last few days, worrying that it might not happen. That sounded right for the Dark Tsar.

'And where the hell are Cam and Shaw?' he said. He was calmer now, pretending to survey the room even as the group still conversed.

Mai came into the room at that moment. It had been her turn to watch the bar area. She caught their eyes and came over.

'It's happened,' she said softly. 'Belgium. Just everyday hospitals caring for their patients. No warning. Many dead and injured. Listen, we have to do anything, *anything,* to get into that room.'

'We were just discussing that,' Alicia said. 'I agree. And we have to do it soon.'

Drake kept his hand close to his gun. 'Soon?' he echoed. 'Yeah, we do it now.'

'Tonight?' Kinimaka asked.

'Yeah, right now. The tsar will be in a partying

mood all night. Look at him. He's happier than a pig in shit. We all try again. We try to get in that room and get close.' Drake wasn't hearing any more about delays. He was going to get this done.

Tonight.

CHAPTER THIRTY SEVEN

Without waiting for a reply, Drake acted. He took hold of Alicia's arm and started walking towards the room. Dahl's hand brought him up short.

'Let Mano and I try first,' he said. 'We're more believable. We've been sitting around on our arses for days with no job. They'll listen to us.'

Drake still saw it as an enormous risk. He hesitated.

'What are you going to do?' Dahl insisted. 'Beg to be on his inner circle list?'

Drake nodded, letting Dahl take the lead. The big Swede immediately turned to Kinimaka and then strode towards the door. Inside, the men were still partying. The TV was still tuned to the tragedy and everyone was still whooping it up and drinking heavily. Drake hadn't planned it this way, but now saw this as the ideal time to make a move.

Dahl knocked loudly. A guard turned to him and then came forward, cupping an ear. He was laughing, though, so Dahl knocked again. This time, three guards approached the door, all with their weapons raised.

One man opened the door and stuck his head out. As soon as the door opened, a wash of noise surged out, mostly laughing and shouting. Drake heard a real party atmosphere.

'What do you want?' the guard yelled.

'The tsar,' Dahl yelled back. 'He promised us jobs. We've been sitting on our arses for days now, doing nothing. I wanna talk to him and find out what's going on.'

'The tsar isn't seeing anyone right now. Come back tomorrow.'

'Hey, I insist,' Dahl said. 'I'm tired of being fucked about.'

The guard stopped looking annoyed and now looked hassled. Clearly he'd had orders from his boss, but now was being forced to defuse a situation. He also didn't want to make a scene or draw too much attention to himself.

'Wait there,' he said. 'I'll ask.'

Dahl put his hand on the door. 'I'd rather ask him myself.'

Now a gun thrust roughly into Dahl's midriff. 'Don't even think about it. You're not getting in here.'

The Swede held his hand up, laughing. 'No need for that,' he said. 'I just want to talk.'

Beside him, Kinimaka was also crowding the doorway. Both men were on the balls of their feet, just waiting to act, waiting for the barest sliver of a chance.

'Like I said, you're not getting in here. Wait there.'

Three guns were trained on Dahl, forcing him to back away.

The guard was as good as his word, walking over to the tsar and asking questions. The tsar looked at Dahl and Kinimaka. At that moment, Dahl straightened, tried to look as though he needed to talk. The tsar nodded in acknowledgement, but didn't beckon him inside. Instead, he waved the guard away and then turned back to his drinks and his friends.

The guard came back to Dahl. 'Nothing for you yet,' he said. 'The tsar says you don't have to stay, but he will need you at some point.'

That was it. Dahl couldn't think of anything else to say. Instead, he glared at the weapons, sighed, and turned away, maintaining his cover. Both he and Kinimaka ambled across to an empty chair and sat themselves down, both looking disconsolate.

Drake wasn't about to wait any longer. He marched up to the door whilst the guards were still there, catching their attention.

'I overheard that,' he said. 'Those guys wanting to see the tsar. Well, my girlfriend and I are guards out here and we're bored as hell. We want in on the tsar's inner circle guard. Can you arrange it?'

The guard looked surprised. So far, there were no guns pointed at Drake, which he took as a win. Beside him, Alicia made herself noticeable by stepping forward. The guard looked at her. 'You two are a package deal, then?'

Drake laughed, keeping it easy. 'It'd be nice.'

The guard turned away, leaving the entrance guarded by the other two. He walked over to the tsar and engaged him in conversation. At first, the tsar shook his head. Drake heard the words, 'Don't need anyone.' But then the tsar appeared to have second thoughts and turned in Drake's and Alicia's direction. There was an evil smile on his lips as his eyes landed firmly on Alicia.

Slowly, he rose to his feet. Instantly, guards

jumped to his side. He made his way through them and came to the door. As he stood there, guards crowded him, guns bristling.

'You want to be part of my special guard?' he asked.

Drake was surprised at having got this far. He was less than six feet from the man, but covered by half a dozen guns, all pointed at his face and heart. 'Yes, sir,' he said finally.

'And you?' the tsar turned to Alicia. 'What do you want with me?'

Drake remembered the tsar's reputation with beautiful women. He hoped Alicia did too, and that she remembered her words – that they should be willing to do anything to get close to the madman.

'I want to guard you closely,' she said, a little suggestively.

The tsar looked at Drake. 'She's your girlfriend?'

Drake nodded. 'We're a package deal. We're better toge-'

But the tsar was no longer listening to him. Instead, he turned back to Alicia.

'You want to get close to me?' he asked.

Alicia gave him a mischievous grin. 'Day and night,' she said.

'You wanna give me a private dance?'

Drake tried to look affronted as the tsar's eyes flicked meanly towards him, a grin on his lips. Alicia turned her expression into a smile.

'Is that what it'll take?'

'A private dance and I'll put both of you on my detail. How's that sound?'

Alicia didn't look at Drake, just held the tsar's

eyes. 'I could do that,' she said. 'If you promise.'

'Oh, I promise, so long as you make it a good one and act like you mean it. Can you do that for me?'

Alicia raised an eyebrow. 'It'll come naturally.'

'I hope so,' he checked his watch. 'But listen, I have a bit of partying to do with my friends before then. How about you come back at eleven?'

Alicia nodded and licked her lips. 'Look forward to it.'

The tsar gave Drake one last sly look and then turned away. The guards immediately shut the door, their faces expressionless. Drake looked at Alicia.

'You're in. You think you can do it?'

'Dance for him? Probably. Kill him? Definitely.'

'It'll all have to be coordinated,' Drake said. 'When you go in and start dancing, we'll start a countdown. Do it all on sixty seconds.'

Alicia nodded. Quickly they did a round of their teammates, explaining the plan. Drake checked the time. It was only 20.45.

'We have time to kill,' he said.

'Then leave it to us to have another go,' Mai said. 'Why wait?'

'You think you can get in there?' Drake asked.

'Look what happened with Alicia. Clearly, he's in the mood. If three beautiful entertainers approach him right now, he won't resist.'

'Don't forget I'm me,' Alicia said, looking Mai up and down. 'And you're... *you*. He might run in terror if you proposition him.'

'We'll get this done,' Hayden said, giving Kinimaka a reassuring smile. 'You just watch.'

'I think that's what *he* wants to do,' Alicia flicked her head in the tsar's direction.

'Good,' Mai said. 'Let him. While he's watching, he'll lose his head.'

CHAPTER THIRTY EIGHT

Hayden, Mai and Kenzie approached the office, knocking at the door. This time, different guards appeared, four of them, all with their guns drawn.

Mai thought about what she wanted to say. She'd rehearsed it a dozen times, but now the chance was here, she felt a little nervous. Especially considering what had recently happened to her boyfriend.

'Yes?' the first guard asked solicitously.

'We'd be damn good as personal waitresses to your boss,' she said. 'Looks like he needs a few.'

The guard looked around. Sure enough, the room was populated entirely by males. The guard looked Mai and the others over. 'You sure you wanna get in amongst all that?'

Mai grinned. 'We're professionals. We'd love it.'

'I don't mean that,' the guard said, trying his best for them. 'They're half drunk, or more than half. They're in song, in heat, in their pig-headedness. Arrogant as fuck,' his voice dropped. 'They'll eat you alive.'

'Still,' Mai was grateful for the guard's attempts to help them, but also determined. 'We see it as a sacrifice to help us get promoted.'

The guard finally shrugged. 'It's your funeral,' he said. 'I'll go ask the boss.'

Mai waited as he crossed the room to the tsar's side, bent over, and asked the question. The tsar looked up, gripping his drink, and turned to look towards the doorway where he saw Mai, Hayden and Kenzie waiting.

His eyes widened.

Mai braced herself for what was about to happen. She sent a surreptitious glance at the others. The tsar rose to his feet and started walking towards the door. If he came within range...

He stopped six feet away. The guards came with him, guns raised.

Mai smiled at the tsar. The man grinned back. 'Tonight's my lucky night,' he said. 'You three want to come inside?'

Mai nodded, and the others stepped forward. She did too, hoping to close the gap. The guards reacted, forcing her to stop. She looked expectantly at the tsar.

'What do you want us to do? In or out?'

The tsar backed away into the room and started back towards his sofa. 'By all means, come in. We'd love to have you.'

This time Mai ignored the guns and entered the room. Hayden and Kenzie followed her. They drifted slowly towards the tsar, who, by now, was sitting cross-legged on his sofa. They had him right where they wanted him.

She took a drinks order, wandered over to the bar and waited for it to be mixed. Hayden and Kenzie did the same, blending in. There were drunken men everywhere, telling stories and jokes and anecdotes. The noise levels were high enough to hurt Mai's eardrums. The TV was blaring too, still tuned to the same channel. As Mai waited, she saw the tsar each out with a remote, switching to some football game. Some men cheered, others booed. The tsar grinned happily and gestured at one of his hangers-on – a tall, bearded individual – and whispered something in that man's ear.

The man looked over at Mai.

He waved to her and then beckoned. Mai's heart leapt. This was it. She delivered the drink in her hand and then walked directly over to the bearded man. She now stood less than six feet from the tsar. A quick look showed three guards closer than her, all with their weapons pointed at the floor. Mai was quick enough to kill in an instant. She just needed the right opportunity.

The bearded man put a hand on her shoulder. 'Tequila on the rocks,' he said. 'For the boss. Better make it a treble.'

Mai nodded and walked away. She would be able to hand it to him. That would be her chance. She walked to the bar, waited for the barman, and gave him her order. A quick glance revealed Hayden being accosted in one corner by a couple of villainous looking individuals, and Kenzie trying to fight off advances to the rear of the room. They were mingling, doing their jobs, blending in and grabbing attention.

Her drink was ready, delivered on a silver platter. She lifted it in one hand and started back towards the table. This was it. The surrounding noise receded as her focus kicked in. Everything turned to slow motion. She drifted through the crowd, caught the eyes of the bearded man, nodded. He nodded slowly back. A thin man hollered right next to her. She didn't react, barely noticed. All her concentration was on the tsar and the distance between them. On what she was going to do when she got close. How she would kill him and then save her own life. The moves she would have to make. Hayden and Kenzie would also be ready. They would be drifting closer, moving behind guards. Ready to act. And out in the main room, Drake and the others would also be in position.

For her well-timed, lethal attack. Coordination was key.

Ten feet separated her from the tsar. Nine... eight...

She kept drifting forward; the drink balanced in her hand. She was six feet from the tsar, as close as she'd ever been. His guards were eyeing her. She made sure they could see the drink. It was a minute loaded with tension that she tried to hide beneath a smile. Her eyes, though – they were as hard as they'd ever been.

Five feet. Four. She came within killing distance. And she wouldn't waste a second. The guards all watched her, and she watched them back, but the tsar was all she wanted. She already knew how she'd kill him.

Hayden and Kenzie waited behind the guards.

Mai was an instant away from unleashing a devastating attack when the tsar suddenly, unexpectedly, surged to his feet. He was yelling, clapping, staring at the TV screen. His guards all reacted instantly – as surprised as Mai – rushing forward with their guns raised. They covered the tsar immediately, even as he cheered.

'Goal!' he yelled.

Guards surrounded Mai, all of them bustling and shoving her out of the way, getting in between her and the tsar. The man himself barely noticed all the activity, so intent was he on the game, but Mai was inundated with guards. And all of them were on edge, wary. She was forced back, out of the way. The bearded man noticed her predicament and came over.

He plucked the glass from the silver platter. 'I'll deliver that for you,' he said.

Mai protested, but he'd already turned away. He made his way through the guards. Mai wondered briefly if she could do the same, but they all turned to stare at him, to check his face before letting him through. It took him an entire minute to reach the tsar.

Mai stood in space. There were at least a dozen bodies now between her and the tsar. And she had been three feet away. But that chance was gone, whisked away by chance. She had been a second away from action.

All around her, the mayhem continued. The shouting. The cheering. The general hubbub. A young man got in her face, leering. She shoved him away, much to his surprise. She felt a hand on her shoulder, another on her waist. Mai pushed them all away, retreated to the quietest corner of the room.

She'd failed. What next?

CHAPTER THIRTY NINE

Drake studied Alicia. 'Are you okay?'
She checked the time. 'Just a little nervous.'
He blinked rapidly. 'You? Are you kidding? I've never known you nervous in you life.'
'Well, how about *you* go dance for the wanker? See how you feel.'
Drake still could hardly believe it. 'Fifteen minutes,' he said. 'You'll be fine, and we're all in place. Mai, Kenzie and Hayden are still in there and will have your back. We'll take care of things out here.'
'Are there enough of you?' Alicia looked dubious.
'Are you kidding? We have the Mad Swede on our side. He'll be happily throwing people left and right before you know it.'
'Then it's all up to me,' Alicia glanced at the tsar's room, which was still a hive of activity. They could make out Mai, Kenzie and Hayden drifting in between patrons, still trying to get close to the tsar, but having no luck. Earlier, Drake and Alicia had been ready for Mai to act, close to three guards, but the chance had never arisen. The moment Mai failed, Drake had felt a terrible shadow descend upon his heart.
Were they ever going to get a stroke of luck?

It didn't feel like it. It felt like they'd been inside the damn castle for months. Their failures so far ate at him.

'Five to eleven,' Alicia said. 'I'd better get ready.'

She took several deep breaths and put her game face on. Drake knew the real Alicia. He could see past her outer façade, and knew that even she had her insecurities. She was the strongest person he knew... at least on the outside.

She winked at him, turned away. Drake watched her go, wracked with conflicting emotion.

Alicia walked up to the room's soundproof door and knocked. A guard came over to her. She yelled out over the wash of noise that emerged with the guard.

'I'm here to see the tsar,' she said. 'Eleven o'clock appointment.' It sounded lame, but she couldn't think of anything else to say.

The man frowned at her. 'You are? He didn't tell me.'

'Just check with him.'

The guy nodded and walked away, locking the door behind him. Alicia watched him walk over to the tsar and lean in. Then, the tsar looked over at her, grinned, and nodded. Alicia swallowed heavily. She could do this, she knew, but she would not like it. The first chance she got to end it, to end him, and she'd take it.

The guard returned, opened the door, and beckoned her in. She gave him her gun, but he still frisked her in a professional manner. Next, he pointed over at the tsar.

'He's all yours.'

Alicia perked up at that. Maybe this wouldn't be so bad after all...

She walked towards the tsar, counting the feet that separated them. As she approached, he rose to his feet. The surrounding conversation died down a notch.

'Hello again,' he said. 'Don't you look good? And where's your boyfriend?'

He was rubbing it in, hoping to taunt her, but it wasn't going to work. She shrugged. 'Out there,' she said. 'Working hard.'

'Good,' the tsar said. 'Well, let's get you working hard, shall we?'

Alicia was made to stop as a guard stepped in between her and the tsar. He shook his head, indicating that six feet was as close as she was going to get. She nodded, knowing that when she danced, he would want her closer.

She went to stand before him, six feet distant, under the watchful eyes of the guards.

'Let's see what you can do,' the tsar said. 'And I'll see if I can get your and your boyfriend a little promotion.'

Alicia forced a smile. She eyed Hayden, Mai and Kenzie, noted that they were in place and ready. She inched forward as close as she dared. 'You got any music?' she asked.

The tsar shook his head. 'Football only,' he said. 'You're gonna have to improvise.' He laughed.

Alicia put her hands on her head and gyrated her hips. There was an immediate cry from the tsar's right. An older, greyer, chunkier individual braying that he wanted her more, that he could offer her more, that the tsar owed him a favour. Alicia tried to ignore him and kept going.

But the man kept on yelling. Eventually, the tsar turned to him. As he did so, Alicia took another step forward, still dancing. Four feet now. The guards, watching her, hadn't noticed.

'Dmitri,' the tsar yelled out. 'You're drunk. I *do* owe you. Do you really want her that much?'

Alicia drifted slightly closer, almost within range now.

'I do!' Dmitri cried out. 'She is my love animal,' he cackled in the way of the manically drunk.

The tsar watched Alicia swivel and twist. She had her hands on her hips and her tongue poking suggestively between her lips. She made sure his entire focus was on her body, not her position in relation to him. All she wanted was for him to hold out his hands, to beckon her into his presence, to reach out.

She could see that he wanted to.

Dmitri yelled out again, showering her with love quotes. She could tell the tsar was becoming more distracted by the second and held out her hands to him. All she needed was for him to do the same.

He looked at her. He opened his mouth to speak. Alicia tensed, ready. The man's life was almost in her hands, and she would end it quickly.

She made that last step, put herself within three feet of the tsar. Now she was in range. She saw Mai and the others tense up. She continued to dance, bunched all her muscles, thought about how she would do it.

The tsar turned to the annoying Dmitri. 'Alright,'

he said. 'Alright, you have her. For God's sake, stop whining and take her.'

Alicia almost froze, but the guards were active now, stepping between her and the tsar. They opened up a route that led directly to Dmitri, the greying man leering horribly. They hadn't noticed what she was about to do, and were just carrying out the tsar's wishes.

'Can't I finish with you first?' Alicia pouted over the shoulder of a guard. 'It won't take long, I promise.'

The tsar stared at her, a kind of longing in his face. Everything hung on a knife's edge. Would he say yes? Would he...

Dmitri bawled out again like a petulant child. The tsar's face closed down. He waved her away. Alicia was herded towards the older man, unable to do anything about it. She cursed inwardly. The old bastard had thwarted all their plans.

She found herself standing before him and performed a perfunctory dance. Maybe she'd get to go back to the tsar afterwards. The older man was too drunk to really care what was happening. He just wanted the attention.

Alicia continued for a short while, and then just melted into the background. Once she was out of the way, the guards didn't seem to care. They left her to her own devices. If she still had her gun, things would be entirely different. Now, though, she looked at Mai and the others. They were still in position.

She drifted back into the tsar's sphere.

'Do you still want that dance?' she yelled, but his attention was off her now. He'd moved on. He waved her away. The guards stared at her impassively. There was no way through. Alicia cursed, and one of the guards smiled, mistaking her reason for being upset. Alicia turned away and went to the bar. She did it because, yes, she needed a drink, but she also did it to signal Drake and the others outside that she'd failed.

Alicia ordered a bourbon, threw in down in one go, and ordered another. In the sixty seconds she stood there, she was hit on twice. Her snarling 'fuck off's' seemed to do the trick.

What next?

So far, everything had failed. They hadn't got close enough. She knew those outside would be even more frustrated, not being able to affect the outcome. The tsar was the most well-protected individual they'd ever come up against.

Was it time for a blitzkrieg? Fuck it all... just go for it.

Alicia wondered what Drake was thinking. It was his decision that had kicked everything off tonight. Was he really going to stand down after all this? She didn't think so.

She stood at the bar and looked out into the main room. Drake was standing to the left, staring right at her as if trying to impart something telepathically. She could see Dahl and Kinimaka hurrying towards him.

Clearly, there was some kind of crisis meeting happening.

Alicia stood ready, prepared to act. She sought the nearest cluster of guards and positioned herself carefully.

CHAPTER FORTY

Drake, feeling powerful frustration, waited for Dahl and Kinimaka to reach him. Trying to keep the emotions off their faces, the three held an intense conversation.

'Nothing's working.' Dahl almost spat. 'We can't get near the bastard.'

They were standing in one corner, facing the tsar's room. Drake could see Alicia watching him and the way she was standing – close to a bunch of guards in the ready position. She was prepared for anything.

Drake looked at his friends. 'We said we'd end this tonight. I think we still have to do that.'

'There's always tomorrow,' Kinimaka said. 'We've failed until now. Doesn't mean we'll fail again tomorrow.'

'We can't try the same thing,' Drake said. 'All the women have tried and failed.'

'But, Mai, Kenzie and Hayden are already in there,' Kinimaka pointed out. 'Maybe tomorrow he'll relax around them. They'll get another chance.'

Drake considered it. Kinimaka's words had some merit. But there was no guarantee the women would be allowed in the tsar's room tomorrow. They couldn't be sure what would happen either way. Drake ground his teeth together. He'd never felt this way before. So frustrated. So inadequate. This was a position they'd never encountered before.

'I... I don't know what to do,' he admitted.

'Risk it,' Dahl growled softly.

Drake blinked at him. 'What?'

'We were going to attack and subdue the guards anyway. We risk it. Go on the offensive, launch an attack. If we can properly surprise them, we can win.'

Drake looked around the room, then into the tsar's abode. 'I'm counting eight guards out here,' he said. 'A further nine in there. You think we can take them all *and* get to the tsar?'

'It's mad,' Kinimaka breathed.

Dahl grinned. 'That's my name. And, yes, I think we can make it work. We're at that juncture now.'

'You're crazy,' Drake said.

'Yes, I am. That's never been a doubt.'

Drake mulled it over. Inside the tsar's room, he could see Alicia and the others were standing in perfect positions to attack from behind, to grab weapons and take out their enemies. Had they anticipated what Dahl wanted to do?

He looked around the room and saw three of the eight guards standing close to a dark corner. Time beat at him with rapid wings. A tough decision had to be made. If they were going to do this, they had to do it now...

Drake didn't hesitate for long. He was used to making snap decisions in the field, even against overwhelming odds, and he made one now. He stared Torsten Dahl in the eye.

'Let's do it,' he said. 'Go mad, but be careful.'

The Swede laughed at his description. Drake

pointed out the guards in the corners of the room. Dahl and Kinimaka chose one and moved off rapidly, getting into position. Drake felt a moment's fear for his team.

Don't let it into your system.

He looked up, caught Alicia's eye. He gave her a nod, wishing he could do more, hoping the gesture would impart their decision. She nodded back. Drake held up five fingers.

Five minutes.

He turned away, walked through the crowd to position himself behind the guard he'd chosen, and waited. He could see both Dahl and Kinimaka and wondered how they'd coordinate this. There wasn't much time to decide.

When they looked his way, he gave them the signal. Now four minutes.

All around him, the party waxed and waned. Looking at the clientele, he saw criminals on every seat, groups of them standing close to the bar and conversing. The noise was relatively muted – these men and women needed to hear themselves speak – but the din of conversation was high. Drake saw a man with a goatee gripping the arm of another, whispering anxiously into his ear. He saw a woman in a black dress, legs crossed, leaning back to talk to her bodyguard, who instantly and forcefully started talking to the man sitting beside her. Everywhere, there was something happening. Only the performers on the stage looked to be content in their element.

Three minutes.

He was ready. He felt confident. Almost the entire team was here, with the exception of Cam and Shaw.

That was a shame, but they would have to cope. The man in front of him shifted position, and Drake did the same.

Two minutes. He tried to make out the women in the tsar's room, saw Hayden and Alicia poised, couldn't make out the others. The atmosphere in there was still raucous, the men entirely distracted. This was the best opportunity they were likely to get.

Into the last minute, and Drake made final preparations. They were risking everything on this attack, even the bombing of the next hospital. Because, if they failed...

It didn't bear thinking about. Drake checked his watch again, counting down the seconds. He rolled his shoulders then bunched his muscles.

Dahl, typically, moved first. He shot his hand out smoothly, wrenched the gun from the guard's hand, and smashed him across his face. A split second later, Kinimaka acted, whipping his own guard's gun away and then punching him hard in the solar plexus. Drake kicked his own guard in the backs of the knees, made him stagger, then stepped around and pulled his gun away before hitting him across the face.

In the tsar's room, Hayden. Alicia, Mai and Kenzie acted simultaneously, attacking the guards and disarming them.

The team was fully focused and harsh as deep winter. They knew these guards willingly protected the worst of the worst and showed them no mercy.

Drake shot his opponent in the chest. Kinimaka did likewise, the gunshots blasting sharply through the hubbub. Dahl got creative, hefted his man across his shoulders and threw him at the room's only window – a stained glass red and black square pane in a far niche. The man hit the window hard, shattering the glass, and went straight through, screaming. Dahl instantly whirled, ready for the next attack.

Drake targeted the room's main guards. They'd killed three, which left five. Two of them were gawping at him. One of those flew backwards, blood spouting from his chest as Kinimaka sighted on him. The other tried to duck behind the sofa, but had the top of his head blown off an instant before he ducked out of sight. It was Dahl's shot, perfectly accurate.

Three guards left in the room.

Now, the initial shock had worn off and people were moving, screaming, trying to get out of the way. Bodyguards were acting for their clients, dragging them down or drawing their own guns. Drake hadn't really factored in the extra bodyguards and hoped they wouldn't start a firefight. This was all about fast acting shock and awe action now – taking out all the enemy before they regrouped.

He moved quickly, targeting another guard. This man was near the bar and Drake suddenly burst out into a sprint, seeing the man targeting him. At the last instant, he threw himself headlong at the man. The two men collided hard and then tumbled over the bar to land behind it.

Drake swung his gun upward, catching the guard underneath the chin. The man's head whipped back, and he grunted, staggering. Drake slammed a fist across his face, heard something crunch, and saw blood spurt from his nose. The guard fell to his knees, but he wasn't done yet.

He still had his gun, and in blinding pain, brought it towards Drake now. The Yorkshireman flung himself to the left as the gun fired; the bullet whistling past his left arm. The problem was – the gun kept firing. The guard had his finger pressed firmly against the trigger. Drake tried to wrestle his own gun up, but he was trapped between the bar and its corner. In the end he was forced to reach out and grab the barrel of the other gun, stopping it from inching its way towards him. This made him vulnerable to a punch, and the guard delivered heavily, targeting Drake's ribs. Drake took the blows, struggling to breathe.

Using all his strength, he rose to his feet, dragging the guard with him. He swiped at the gun, knocking it from the man's hand, and then pushed him back against the bar. Bottles wobbled and then smashed down all around him, shattering their contents all over the floor. There was a waterfall of liquor and the bottles rained down and broke across his skull, blinding him. He was covered in broken glass and disorientated.

Drake brought his gun up and shot him. Blood mixed with neat alcohol and pooled across the floor as the man went down.

Dahl and Kinimaka took the other two remaining guards. Dahl vaulted over the sofa his opponent was hiding behind and planted two feet in the man's chest, sending him tumbling back. The man lost his grip on his gun as he rolled, unable to arrest his own momentum. Dahl landed and aimed his weapon at the man's centre mass.

Pulled the trigger.

Kinimaka traded shots with the last guard, ducking behind a plush leather chair. When one of the guard's bullets penetrated the chair entirely, slicing past Kinimaka's face, he changed tactics. He rose, firing constantly as he ran towards the guard's hiding place, creating his own cover. He leapt over, coming down on top of the guard with a heavy elbow. The blow came down on the top of the man's skull, felling him. But he wasn't done immediately. He squirmed, coughing, grunting, trying to bring his weapon to bear. Kinimaka stomped down on his head.

The man stopped moving.

And suddenly, Drake, Dahl and Kinimaka were looking at each other. They'd taken care of the guards.

But now there were other dangers in the room.

CHAPTER FORTY ONE

Alicia hit hard when the time came. She punched her guard in the throat and then his eyes, making him scream, grabbed his gun and twisted it out of his hands. Immediately, she turned the barrel on another guard and blew him away. To her left and right, Hayden, Mai, and Kenzie were doing similar things. Gunshots rang through the room.

The tsar hit the floor quickly. His close guard fell around him, shielding him with their bodies. Other men dropped to their knees, taking cover, still in shock but trying to locate a target.

Alicia couldn't help but give them one. She stood there firing toward the tsar, hoping to take him out quickly, but either her bullets missed or they didn't penetrate his shield of guards. After a few seconds, she had to move as the guards targeted her.

Alicia dived behind the bar, hoping it was made of something substantial. She landed on her shoulder, bruising the bone, and yelled out, almost dropped her gun but managed to hold on to it. Bullets slammed into the bar, none of them making it through. The sound of splintering wood and thudding metal filled her ears.

Hayden raced across the room, leaping at a guard and taking him by the throat. She squeezed hard. He punched at her, trying to aim his gun at her, but lacking the room. With her free hand, she punched his solar plexus and then his nose, blinding him with tears. Another punch and the man staggered, almost falling to his knees. She plucked his back-up handgun from his waist and shot him with it. The man went down.

Swivelling, she targeted another guard who was shooting at Kenzie, shot him in the back. Then she moved, creating a hard target.

Kenzie also fired into the bunch of guards protecting the tsar. She saw blood blossom across a chest, saw a man get shot in the arm. One guard didn't move again, but another rose, firing back at her. Kenzie flinched as bullets flew past her skull, inches away. She hit the deck, rolling to another position. By her count, there were only six guards left in the room and several other clients.

And the tsar.

She clambered up over a dead guard, targeting the next man.

* * *

Drake had been assessing the battle even as he fought. There were two new guards out here. As Kinimaka and Dahl fired at them, keeping them down, Drake broke into a sprint. He couldn't use his gun because his target was standing behind a marble pillar, but he could get close on the man's blind side. He ran right up to the pillar and aimed his gun around it.

The man saw him, grunted, and grabbed Drake's

gun arm. He forced it downward, negating the weapon. Drake struggled with the man, who was strong, the pair grabbing hold of each other. Now they were fighting hand to hand, too close for Kinimaka or Dahl to try a shot.

Drake backed up, right into a metal pole. It was solid and thick, the same one the dancers had been using earlier. He saw stars as he took a punch to the face. At the same time, he struggled to bring his gun up, to no avail. In the end, he forgot about the gun and tried to yank his way out of the other guy's grip. He struck the pole again, his boots loud on the stage floor. The guard swiftly brought his gun up.

And Drake fell to his knees, suddenly free. He slipped around the pole, then punched out, striking the other man's thighs and groin. There was a loud grunt, and the man folded. Drake grabbed hold of the back of his head and smashed it into the pole. There was a loud clunk, and the man fell to the floor, sinking into oblivion. Drake couldn't leave an unconscious enemy behind, not today, so shot him in the head.

One guard left. Dahl focused on him. But it wasn't just the guards they had to watch now. The scattered clients' bodyguards were targeting the team too, thinking they were a threat. Kinimaka had already shouted at them, telling them they were just here for the tsar, but most of the bodyguards didn't take him at face value, not surprisingly. Some of them probably didn't even know who the so-called tsar was.

Dahl picked up a glass table and hurled it in the direction of the last guard. The object flew through the air, arcing high. Dahl ran after it. The table struck the guard's hiding place and shattered with a loud bang, glass exploding everywhere. The guard ducked low, probably wondering what the hell was happening. As he did, Dahl flung himself at the cowering man, striking him at shoulder height.

The man was bowled over, falling headlong. Dahl landed on top of him and wasted no time ending the threat.

Drake was watching the doors to the main room, knowing other guards might appear at any moment. When they did, he let them enter the room and then sent a spray of bullets at them, cutting them down. So far, he'd killed four newcomers.

The three men rose to their feet, looking now at the door to the tsar's room. Before he could act, Drake was accosted by a scrawny-looking man, one of the many criminals in the room, who came at him with a broken bottle. Drake shook his head wearily, grabbed the bottle arm, and broke it. Then he shot the man in the stomach.

'Back off, arseholes,' he yelled out clearly. 'We told you. We're not here for you. We're only here for the tsar.'

'Fuck you!' one man yelled back, drew his weapon and tried to fire a shot. Before he squeezed the trigger, Dahl had shot him through the left eye, leaving a large smoking hole. The man rolled back, dead, his figure proving a deterrent to the other assembled criminals. Drake waved Dahl and Kinimaka towards the door.

'Time to end this,' Drake said.

***

Inside the room, Alicia was crawling among dead bodies. They'd taken out four of the tsar's guards by now and they were littered across the floor. They also provided great shields. Alicia jerked as she felt a bullet enter one of the dead bodies, the vibrations passing through to her own, unsettling her. She targeted the shooter, narrowly missing his forehead.

People were scattered everywhere. The tsar had not been moved, now lying under four protective bodies. The spare guard was kneeling close by, trying and failing to target all the attackers. He was the most vulnerable for now, and if she could take him out, it would force one of the others to leave the tsar's side. They couldn't all just lie there, covering him and doing nothing else.

Alicia crawled faster, gaining a new position. To her right, Kenzie and Mai crouched behind a wide marble pedestal. When the statue above them wobbled after being hit by a bullet, they made to dive away, but it settled before falling. The battle had hit a kind of stalemate.

And yet Alicia knew it couldn't stay that way. The longer it went on, the greater the odds fell in the tsar's favour. She made a decision, grabbed a discarded gun, and hurled it in the guard's direction. When he looked up distractedly, moving to one side, she rose and fired three times. Her bullets smashed into his collarbone, sending him hurtling backwards, already dead.

Which left four guards.

But others in the room weren't cowering any

longer. They were angry and upset. They were arrogant and full of themselves, terribly affronted that anyone would start a firefight in their presence. One of these men, an obese Russian with a bald head, ordered his two guards to immediately kill Alicia and the others. He said it in a way that he expected no resistance on behalf of the women.

The two bodyguards drew their weapons and started firing. Bullets flashed through the air all around Alicia and she ducked, grinding her body into the ground. The flesh around her took several hits, the bodies jerking.

Only when the shooting paused for the men to reload did she raise her head. But she wasn't fast enough. Before she could shoot, Mai and Kenzie had done the job for her, firing from behind the marble pillar. The bodyguards fell and the obese Russian was also hit in the skull, the back of his head exploding. One of the other criminals, who had been looking like he might follow the Russian's lead, immediately backed down and sank further into his hiding place.

Alicia swivelled as she heard a commotion at the door. Drake and the others were coming through. As he came, Drake swivelled and fired a tracery of shots at the entrance to the room, taking down three newcomers. The men danced in agony and then went down hard, bleeding all over the floor.

Dahl and Kinimaka flew into the room, diving for cover.

Clearly, there was talk among the tsar's bodyguards for now they all leapt up, kneeling in front of their cowering boss, and opened fire. Salvos of bullets laced the air, the sound of intense gunfire filling the room.

It was the tsar's last stand.

And then he rose up too, machine gun in hand.

CHAPTER FORTY TWO

Drake rolled into the room, taking cover behind the corner of the bar, hoping it was made of the same material as the one outside. Bullets smashed into it and didn't penetrate, allowing him a sigh of relief. He checked the guns he'd picked up on the way to the room, saw them almost completely full.

Dahl and Kinimaka were in front of him, one ducked behind a support pillar, the other crouched behind a solid-looking table that had been upturned. Their barriers were being struck constantly by bullets, but at this rate the guards were going to run out fast.

They seemed to realise it too and stopped firing. Without a moment's pause, Dahl and Kinimaka reached around and fired their weapons, aiming at the exposed men. For now, they missed, but the guards were in a vulnerable position, and it was only a matter of time. The tsar also dropped low, his machine gun resting across his lap.

Drake could see everyone from his position at the back of the room. He saw they were all in good cover positions. A heavy silence suddenly fell, even deeper after the gunfire, and he could hear several people breathing.

'What do you want of me?' the tsar yelled out. 'What is going on?'

Drake debated whether to answer, but the bastard didn't deserve a reply. He deserved to die in ignorance. Drake answered his plea with a bullet that flashed close to one of his guards. Around the room, other men whispered and groaned and growled softly.

Now they had entered a bit of a stalemate. Drake and his team were pinned down despite their superior numbers. The guards were clustered together with the tsar at the centre, but they were heavily armed. And the longer this went on, the better for the tsar. He looked around for inspiration.

And his eyes fell on Torsten Dahl.

The Mad Swede was quietly lifting the big table he was hiding behind. He had both hands underneath it and was now flexing his knees, lifting it off the floor. With a huge grunt, he hefted it and then paused, glanced back at Drake.

'Ready?'

Drake nodded. Some of the others saw what was about to happen, but some didn't. Never mind, they would soon catch on when Dahl acted.

Which was instantly. The Swede roared as he straightened and then started running with the table held out before him for cover. He covered the distance quickly, but not before several bullets had struck the surface, pounding the hard metal. The Swede's muscles were straining hard, his biceps bulging. His legs pumped. Luckily, there were no obstacles in his way. He slammed into the guards as they stood firing, smashing the upturned table into them. Two of them leapt away, but the other two were struck hard and went sprawling.

Drake was running Dahl's wake, and then the others came out of hiding. Soon, the entire team was sprinting behind Dahl, converging on their enemy. Drake noticed the amazing sight out of the corner of his eye: the complete team attacking, yelling, trying to right the terrible wrong that was the Dark Tsar.

Dahl stumbled as the table fell from his hands and came down on two of the guards. The other two rose and attacked him, but then Drake arrived. Smashed one across the back of the head. Alicia grappled with the other; the two of them went sprawling to the ground.

Dahl clambered over the table and went for the two guards he'd downed.

The rest of the team arrived, punching, kicking, taking out the last of the tsar's guard. When three other men stepped forward, clients of the tsar hoping to help him out, Mai whirled and backhanded one across the face. She front kicked him and then spun, kicking him in the chin. The man went down hard. Still spinning, she stepped into the next man, taking him off Kenzie because she really wanted to hurt people, to help assuage the pain she felt. This time she leapt up mid spin and kicked her opponent in the throat. The guy didn't even have time to yelp. Finally, she swept the floor with her trailing leg, tripped the third attacker and watched him hit the floor with his spine. When he landed, she came down on his head with her knee, knocking him unconscious.

Three attackers taken out in seconds by one person.

This gave anyone else who'd been considering helping the tsar pause. They now looked on, staying in cover. It was Hayden and Kinimaka who targeted the tsar himself. As Dahl, Drake, and Alicia handled his guards, the man raised his weapon. He took aim. As he did so, Hayden fired. Her bullet slammed into the tsar's gun and sent it spinning from his hands. Kinimaka ran up to him and slapped him across the face.

The tsar looked shocked and affronted. Kinimaka didn't stand on ceremony. He repeated the slap. The tsar came at him then, all legs and fists, striking out. Kinimaka took the blows, standing his ground, blocking most of them. The tsar was going red in the face, yelling as he pummelled the big Hawaiian.

Around him, the last of his men fell. The tsar was left very much alone, facing the Ghost Squadron.

Drake still knew that they needed to end this quickly. No more guards had entered the main room yet, so he was relatively confident they'd got them all, but there still might be a few stragglers.

He turned his attention to the tsar.

'You're done,' he said. 'Finished. Now make it easy on yourself and tell us where the last four bombs are.'

The tsar sneered at them. 'I will tell you nothing. Do your worst.'

Drake was about to do exactly that, but Mai stepped in. She jabbed the tsar in the solar plexus and then gripped his throat in two fingers, squeezing hard. The tsar started choking, his knees buckling. Mai didn't let up. She let the man fall to his knees, maintaining eye contact. Finally, the man's hands came up to grab her wrists pleadingly.

Mai let go. The tsar almost collapsed, but

managed to hold himself up. The man coughed and gasped as he tried to speak. 'You... you infiltrated my... my organisation. Did you have two others?'

Drake frowned. 'What?'

'Did you have two others with you? Cam and Shaw?'

'What about them?' Hayden asked.

All this time, Kinimaka and Dahl were keeping their eyes on the other occupants of the room, making sure they attempted nothing stupid.

'I have them, or what's left of them. I'll trade you my life for theirs.'

Drake saw red. This bastard was murdering hundreds of innocent people every week. He was bombing hospitals. And here he was, bartering for his freedom, trying to trade two lives for it. He reached out, gripped the top of the man's head, and put his thumb close to his left eye.

'Tell me where they are,' he said. 'Or lose an eye.'

The tsar scowled at him. Drake jabbed his thumb into the man's eye and started to push hard. The tsar screamed. He tried to pull away, but Drake's grip was too strong. Drake felt the eyeball move under the pressure, dug in harder.

'Stop, stop, please stop.' The tsar yelled. 'They are with Javier in the blue room.' He gave them directions. 'Please leave my eye alone.'

Drake turned to Dahl, Kinimaka, and Mai. 'Cam and Shaw,' he said. 'Get them back.'

And then he turned back to the tsar. 'Now,' he said. 'Let's talk about those hospitals.'

* * *

Dahl, Kinimaka and Mai ran from the room, following the tsar's directions. They raced along a corridor, took the first right, and found themselves facing a blue door. Dahl didn't slow, didn't pause for a second, didn't even check to see if it was unlocked. He hit it at full speed, crashing through.

Kinimaka and Mai flew in his wake, backing him up.

They smashed their way into the blue room. Inside it was spacious, with stark strip lights, a long bench to the left covered with implements, and several chairs and tables. The room held an atmosphere of despair, as if this was a place where things went to die.

Facing them, tied to chairs, were Cam and Shaw. Their heads were down, their chins resting on their chests. Blood coated their clothing. Mai could clearly see that at least one of Cam's arms was broken, maybe both. Shaw appeared not to have fared much better. Blood dripped off their bodies, pooling on the floor.

Were they alive?

Also facing them was a bald man. He held a handgun and was pointing it at them. Mai instantly raised her own gun. Javier went to stand behind Cam and Shaw, making himself a harder target.

'Cam?' Dahl said. 'Shaw? You okay?'

Javier sneered. 'Don't move,' he said. 'Or you'll be as dead as they are.'

Both Dahl and Kinimaka now also had the bald man in their sights. They inched forward, advancing further into the room.

'Cam?' Dahl tried again. 'Shaw?'

No response. No movement at all.

Javier waved his gun at them. 'Lower your-'

Dahl's bullet smashed through his forehead at eight hundred miles per hour. The man had made the mistake of waving his weapon, losing sight for a split second. That mistake had cost him his life.

As Javier flew backwards, already dead, Kinimaka and Mai rushed towards Cam and Shaw. Mai reached Shaw first and checked for a pulse. It was there, but it was weak. She turned to Kinimaka.

'He's alive,' he said with relief. 'But they're both pretty banged up.'

Dahl came up and nodded towards Javier. 'But they're both better off than that asshole,' he said.

CHAPTER FORTY THREE

They called the relevant authorities and waited for armed men to come out to the castle. They spent hours and days explaining who they were, what they were doing, and how they'd tracked down the tsar. They kept Michael Crouch's name out of it, but came clean with everything else. As they were interviewed, the final hospital bombs were found, which went a long way to verifying their authenticity. Still, to Drake, it felt like a long time before they were finally released, finally on their way home.

They left on a military plane along with Cam and Shaw and two nurses who were caring for the couple. On their way to DC, they sat as close to their friends as they could, not wanting to let them be alone. Cam had a broken collarbone and a broken arm. Shaw had a broken arm and ankle. Both had suffered lacerations to their bodies and severe bruising. They would be out of action for months. The tsar's men had really done a number on them. When they finally woke up at the hospital, the team had been standing there waiting for them, smiles on their faces.

Now, they were sedated for the long flight back to DC.

Drake, sitting beside Alicia, wasn't entirely sure how he felt. It had been a long, hard mission, different from what they were used to. He felt they hadn't done enough, that they hadn't won entirely. Yes, they had unmasked and bagged the Dark Tsar. They had destroyed his entire operation, saving people all around the world. Even so, bombs had gone off and many had been killed. They were a day late to stop the third bombing.

Had they really won the day?

Not for those who had died. So Drake sat there, mixed feelings inside, not wanting to be happy but not wanting to feel sad. And judging by the looks on the faces of his friends, they felt exactly the same way.

'I don't know how I feel,' he tried to explain. 'We beat the tsar, got everything we wanted, but it feels like we lost.'

The low hum of the plane counterpointed his words. There was no other sound as the team stared at each other.

'Maybe it's these two,' Hayden said, nodding at Cam and Shaw in their beds. 'Our team isn't intact. We didn't get through it unscathed. Not even close.'

'They will recover,' Alicia said.

'In time,' Dahl said. 'They're in a bad way. And we were all part of the decision that got them captured.'

'We didn't win,' Mai said quietly. 'Not this time. We lost Bryant. We almost lost Cam and Shaw. Six hospitals got bombed.'

Drake was feeling vulnerable. He reached out for Alicia and gave her a hug. All around him, the others continued to stare with glum expressions.

'But we did take down the tsar,' Dahl attempted to lighten the mood. 'We can claim that as a victory.'

'He was a nightmare in more ways than one,' Hayden said. 'The world is a better place now.'

Drake knew they were right, but the sight of Cam and Shaw, the memory of Bryant's death, the knowledge of those hospitals – it all weighed him down.

'You know,' Hayden said. 'There's nothing we can do about our failings. We move on. You know where we're going, right?'

'Home,' Alicia said, and it felt right to her. They had lived in DC long enough by now to call it home. In any case, it was as close to home as they were going to get. They were travellers of the world, never in one place for too long, always seeking the next job.

'Home,' Hayden agreed. 'But that's not entirely what I meant. We're going back to a new way forward. To a new life. A new future. Don't you remember?'

Drake did now. The thought gave him a little lift.

'The private security firm,' Hayden said. 'The new company.'

'It's gonna change things,' Kenzie said.

'For the better,' Kinimaka put in. 'At least I hope so.'

'When I mentioned it to Michael, he said he'd help us out as much as possible,' Drake said. 'By putting our name forward. Getting us started. That kind of thing. He'll help with contacts. There won't be any shortage of jobs.'

'And we can cover for Cam and Shaw until they're up and about again,' Dahl said.

The thought of the new future helped Drake. It made him feel marginally better about going forward. There was opportunity, something new, something they could build on. He wondered what the next few months with his friends would bring.

'I like the thought of something new,' Alicia said. 'I wonder where the road will take us.'

Away from here, Drake thought.

'I'm already looking forward to it,' Hayden said.

Drake smiled at his friends. The future stretched out before them like a long, winding opportunity-strewn road, vanishing into the distance. It might not be laden with diamonds, but it was sprinkled with potential.

And it was exactly what he needed.

THE END

Thank you for purchasing and reading the latest Matt Drake. I really hope you enjoyed it and I'm looking forward to taking the team in a new direction when the series continues. Next up, it will be the new Joe Mason – **The Traitor's Gold** – to be released on 6th June, already available for pre-order. If you enjoyed this book, please leave a rating or a review. Many thanks!

If you enjoyed this book, please leave a review or a rating.

DAVID LEADBEATER

Other Books by David Leadbeater:

The Matt Drake Series
A constantly evolving, action-packed romp based in the escapist action-adventure genre:

The Bones of Odin (Matt Drake #1)
The Blood King Conspiracy (Matt Drake #2)
The Gates of Hell (Matt Drake 3)
The Tomb of the Gods (Matt Drake #4)
Brothers in Arms (Matt Drake #5)
The Swords of Babylon (Matt Drake #6)
Blood Vengeance (Matt Drake #7)
Last Man Standing (Matt Drake #8)
The Plagues of Pandora (Matt Drake #9)
The Lost Kingdom (Matt Drake #10)
The Ghost Ships of Arizona (Matt Drake #11)
The Last Bazaar (Matt Drake #12)
The Edge of Armageddon (Matt Drake #13)
The Treasures of Saint Germain (Matt Drake #14)
Inca Kings (Matt Drake #15)
The Four Corners of the Earth (Matt Drake #16)
The Seven Seals of Egypt (Matt Drake #17)
Weapons of the Gods (Matt Drake #18)
The Blood King Legacy (Matt Drake #19)
Devil's Island (Matt Drake #20)
The Fabergé Heist (Matt Drake #21)
Four Sacred Treasures (Matt Drake #22)
The Sea Rats (Matt Drake #23)
Blood King Takedown (Matt Drake #24)

Devil's Junction (Matt Drake #25)
Voodoo soldiers (Matt Drake #26)
The Carnival of Curiosities (Matt Drake #27)
Theatre of War (Matt Drake #28)
Shattered Spear (Matt Drake #29)
Ghost Squadron (Matt Drake #30)
A Cold Day in Hell (Matt Drake #31)
The Winged Dagger (Matt Drake #32)
Two Minutes to Midnight (Matt Drake #33)
The Devil's Reaper (Matt Drake#34)

The Alicia Myles Series
Aztec Gold (Alicia Myles #1)
Crusader's Gold (Alicia Myles #2)
Caribbean Gold (Alicia Myles #3)
Chasing Gold (Alicia Myles #4)
Galleon's Gold (Alicia Myles #5)
Hawaiian Gold (Alicia Myles #6)

The Torsten Dahl Thriller Series
Stand Your Ground (Dahl Thriller #1)

The Relic Hunters Series
The Relic Hunters (Relic Hunters #1)
The Atlantis Cipher (Relic Hunters #2)
The Amber Secret (Relic Hunters #3)
The Hostage Diamond (Relic Hunters #4)
The Rocks of Albion (Relic Hunters #5)
The Illuminati Sanctum (Relic Hunters #6)
The Illuminati Endgame (Relic Hunters #7)

The Atlantis Heist (Relic Hunters #8)
The City of a Thousand Ghosts (Relic Hunters #9)
Hierarchy of Madness (Relic Hunters #10)

The Joe Mason Series
The Vatican Secret (Joe Mason #1)
The Demon Code (Joe Mason #2)
The Midnight Conspiracy (Joe Mason #3)
The Babylon Plot (Joe Mason #4)
The Traitor's Gold (Joe Mason #5)

The Rogue Series
Rogue (Book One)

The Disavowed Series:
The Razor's Edge (Disavowed #1)
In Harm's Way (Disavowed #2)
Threat Level: Red (Disavowed #3)

The Chosen Few Series
Chosen (The Chosen Trilogy #1)
Guardians (The Chosen Trilogy #2)
Heroes (The Chosen Trilogy #3)

Short Stories
Walking with Ghosts (A short story)
A Whispering of Ghosts (A short story)

DAVID LEADBEATER

All genuine comments are very welcome at:

davidleadbeater2011@hotmail.co.uk

Twitter: @dleadbeater2011

Visit David's website for the latest news and information:
davidleadbeater.com

Printed in Great Britain
by Amazon